SSLgs

W9-CEY-418

This Large Print Book carries the
Seal of Approval of N.A.V.H.

Song
of the
Prairie

Esther Loewen Vogt

Thorndike Press • Thorndike, Maine

Published in 1998 by arrangement with Christian Publications.

Thorndike Large Print ® Christian Fiction Series.

The tree indicium is a trademark of Thorndike Press.

The text of this Large Print edition is unabridged.
Other aspects of the book may vary from the original edition.

Set in 16 pt. Plantin by Juanita Macdonald.

Printed in the United States on permanent paper.

Library of Congress Cataloging in Publication Data

Vogt, Esther Loewen.
    Song of the prairie / Esther Loewen Vogt.
      p.   cm.
    ISBN 0-7862-1490-2 (lg. print : hc : alk. paper)
    1. Large type books.   2. Marriage — Kansas — Fiction.
  3. Frontier and pioneer life — Fiction.   4. Christian fiction.
  I. Title.
    [PS3572.O3S58   1998]
    813'.54—dc21   98-4373

DEDICATION

To my sisters Rosena and Rosella, identical twins (like biblical characters Tryphena and Tryphosa), who are "women who work hard in the Lord" (Romans 16:12). They have put up with me, loved me and supported my writing through many years. To them I dedicate this book.

Trust in the LORD with all thine heart;
  and lean not unto thine own understanding.
In all thy ways acknowledge him,
  and he shall direct thy paths.
(Proverbs 3:5–6, KJV)

Author Note

For readers like me who like to have fact and fiction sorted out, I offer the following.

Council Grove played a unique role in early Kansas history. No other town in the state has held a special place in the colorful history and has been called the "peerless city of the plains." The name Council Grove originated from treaty negotiations conducted in a grove of oak trees in 1825. The treaty, forged between U.S. Commissioners and Osage Indian chiefs, granted white travelers safe passage along the Santa Fe Trail.

Nestled beside the Neosho River, the town provided a comfortable camping and meeting place with its ample shade, water and grass for native Americans, explorers, soldiers and Santa Fe travelers. The Kaws (or Kansa Indians for which the state was named) lived in tepee villages south of the town from 1847 until 1873.

Seth M. Hays, Council Grove's first white settler, established his home and trading post west of the Neosho River. He was a great grandson of Daniel Boone. Kit Carson was his cousin. In 1850 the Methodist Episcopal Church South established a mission and school for the Kaws. The building of native stone stood two stories tall with eight rooms and was designated to accommodate 50 students. It served as Indian school and mission until 1866. This building still stands and is used as a museum.

Early day features of the town included the Brown Jug which served as a schoolhouse and community center for elections, town meetings, chautauquas and other public events. It was also used as a church building and union Sunday school for all denominations until each church erected its own edifice.

Famous characters visited the town from time to time, such as Susan B. Anthony, Elisabeth Cady Stanton, General George Custer and Governor Robinson. Several notorious persons such as outlaw Jack McDowell and the lawless Dick Yeager Gang also were a part of Council Grove's early history.

The "alarm bell" arrived in town from Lawrence via ox team in 1866. For about 40 years it was used as a school and church bell and as an alarm for Indian attacks and fires.

Another unique feature of Council Grove was the Hermit's Cave, named for the "hermit priest of the Santa Fe Trail," as he was called. He made his home for about five months in a small cave carved into the side of the cliff above the Neosho. Later the cave was used by young lovers as a secret "post office." Here they left love letters to each other in its craggy crevices. The cave is still accessible.

The Cheyenne Indian attack on June 3, 1868, was a frightening event. Through courage and faith in God, the town was spared. Historical research about the raid is accurate.

It is in Council Grove, set in 1867-69, that I place my fictitious characters Annamarie Tate and Brad Bennett, who have been driven apart through misunderstandings and tragedy.

During the late 1860s, Plains Indian raids across the western third of Kansas intensified as they murdered new settlers, kidnapped women and children and set fire to their farms and ranches, especially in the Saline and Solomon Valleys. Angry because the white men were stealing their buffalo lands, the Cheyennes were out for revenge.

Since the government in Washington had obviously ignored the problem, Generals Sherman and Custer decided to subdue the marauding bands. Most of the 2,600 soldiers were occupied with protecting the wagon trains along the Santa Fe Trail and the construction workers on the Union Pacific Railroad, and thus the settlers were left unprotected.

Colonel Forsythe was ordered to organize a troop of 50 volunteer scouts to pursue the roving bands. Camped along the banks of the Arickaree Fork of the Republican River, this small band was surprised by a horrendous charge of Cheyenne warriors under Chief Roman Nose. Hemmed in on three sides, the soldiers were forced to scramble for shelter on a small island in the Arickaree River where they fought valiantly. The Cheyennes recklessly charged this small cavalry time after time, and the cavalry met charge after charge. Finally two scouts slipped through enemy lines and hurried to Fort Wallace 90 miles away for reinforcements. During the fifth charge, Roman Nose was killed. The Indians began to retreat after their leader had fallen. It is in this setting that Brad Bennett in the story volunteers to help make the prairies safer for Kansas settlers.

Minor roles are played by actual historical figures. The story is set in this historical background and is seen through Annamarie's eyes. It is through her deep faith in God that the story reaches a satisfying climax.

If it has deviated from historical facts, it is no less strange than the facts themselves, which were sometimes vague in my research. Thus, this novel is a work of fiction, but based on fact and used fictitiously.

Esther Loewen Vogt
Hillsboro, Kansas

CHAPTER 1

"Do you hear the Overland, Emmy Lou? It seems I've waited forever!"

Annamarie Tate stood in the doorway of the inn called Hays House and paused to listen again. The warm October breeze lifted the brown curls that feathered around her heart-shaped face and framed its dewy freshness with the glow of late afternoon.

Emmy Lou Hanks wrinkled her freckled nose and laughed. "I guess you're more anxious to see Bradford Bennett than the Overland! Of course, he's been gone for a few years —"

"Three. He left right after Lee surrendered, and by now he should've learned all they could teach him about banking in that fancy Ohio college." She poised herself on tiptoe and peered to the east where the Santa Fe Trail snaked its dusty way toward Council Grove's main street.

"Well," Emmy Lou touched Annamarie's blue-checked shoulder, "I missed you while you were gone, too."

"Mother and Father felt I needed some

social graces along with the academy courses so I lived with Grandma and Grandpa Lipscombe in Illinois. But it hardly seems I've been back since August. I wonder if Brad —" she paused and moved to lean against the hitching rail.

"If Brad what, Annamarie? Still likes you?" Emmy Lou was at her elbow.

Annamarie's dark blue eyes sparkled. "He always said I was his girl and asked me to wait for him. He never was much of a letter-writer, though. But he always said someday he . . . we . . . well, I just hope he hasn't forgotten! Since he's been away, who knows? Some gorgeous girl could've stolen his heart."

"Gorgeous girl!" Emmy Lou snorted as she flipped a mousy brown braid over her shoulder. "I can't think of anyone more gorgeous than Annamarie Tate. You've become a woman since he left. You're no longer a giddy teenager, and if he's fallen for someone else, he needs to have his eyes examined."

Annamarie laughed, her voice a trilling tinkle. "Too bad Council Grove hasn't lured an eye doctor to set up practice." She caught a glimpse of her own reflection in the dusty windowpane of the inn. She noticed her adorably dimpled chin, but she thought her mouth was too wide and her nose was too abrupt for her to be considered beautiful.

She had been 14 and Brad was 16 when he went away. He was tall and muscular even then, and his hair was thick and brown with just a hint of curl. She'd never seen eyes a deeper brown. They'd reminded her of a collie's. His arms had already been sinewy and strong three years ago. Now he was 19 and she was 17. Would Brad Bennett have changed? She turned her gaze back to Emmy Lou.

"Didn't Brad's father want him to join him in his bank?" Emmy Lou asked.

"Those were his plans," Annamarie said. "Of course, it's not a real bank yet but they do make bank loans."

Although Emmy Lou would never win a beauty contest, she was a gentle and loyal friend to Annamarie, and the two girls had known each other since their families had moved to Council Grove in 1853 from Illinois.

During the Civil War the fighting had seemed so remote to this rugged Kansas town. Most boys had been too young to fight, although a few fathers had gone to help the cause, which, of course, was on the Union side in Free State Kansas.

Frank Keitch had tried to enlist but was turned down because of poor eyesight. Their crowd — Ed Keitch, Jeremy Jackson, Sally Brown, Dave and Paula Briggs and Emmy Lou and Annamarie — would be complete again when Brad returned. They were a close-knit group who especially enjoyed singing, fun and games. It would be good to have Brad back.

Annamarie smiled, remembering. She and Brad had often sung together in church because their voices "blended like warm honey," Uncle Chris Baxter always said. Would Brad ask her to sing with him again? Tonight was prayer meeting at the Brown Jug. If Brad was on today's stage coach, he'd probably be back in time.

I mustn't appear too eager, she told herself. *Besides, my face will burn brown if I stand out here in the sun too long.*

The October sun was still warm although the nights were brisk with chill of autumn. She stepped back into the shade of the overhang and sighed.

Emmy Lou stared at her. "Are you sure Brad's on this stage, Annamarie?"

"It's the only one due this week. His letter said he'd come the week of October 18."

"So he's written to you?" Emmy Lou wiped the dampness from her freckled face.

Annamarie grinned. "If you call his brief scribbled notes letters. His writing is atro-

18

cious. He should've studied to be a doctor!"
She laughed again.

"Listen . . . I think I hear faint rattle. Oh,
yes, there's a cloud of dust far up the Trail."
Emmy Lou cocked her head to listen.

"The Kaws will no doubt welcome the
passengers, as usual. At least their tribe has
not caused us any trouble," Annamarie said
as an excited tingle ran down her spine. "I
still can't understand why they're so in-
trigued by a stage coach."

"Perhaps it's because it's so different from
a covered wagon. Why not ask your friend,
Po-a-be?" Emmy Lou said, standing on tiptoe. "After all, she's one of your special
friends."

"Yes. Both of you are. Po-a-be *is* special.
She was one Kaw who came every day to
the Mission school, and I'm glad she learned
to speak good English. Many resisted being
taught 'white man ways,' you know."

"Is she a Kaw? Somehow she doesn't look
like the others."

"I believe she's part Osage. Or she might
be a Hopi. But she's been on the Kaw reservation for a good while. Indians often join
other tribes." Annamarie paused.

The stage coach was slowing now as it
neared the town. She stepped back into the
doorway to wait for its arrival. The clatter of

horses' hooves on the hard-packed trail grew more distinct, and eagerness lit her blue eyes. She *had* waited for Brad as he'd asked her to, and now she could scarcely wait until the stage drew up so she could see him again.

When it rolled to a stop with a rattle of dry leaves in a cloud of dust, Annamarie leaned against the doorjam of the tavern. She saw the heads of several passengers through the stage windows. Would Brad be one of them?

Finally, after a hoarse yell from the driver the passengers began to appear. A buxom, black-gowned woman and a man with a handle-bar mustache hopped from the stage. Then Annamarie saw *them* — Bradford Bennett — and the blond. She noticed how carefully he helped her from the stage and took her arm as he led her toward the inn. The girl was tall and slim with hair like fine spun taffy. Her eyes were a smoldering green. She clung to Brad's arm with one hand as she smoothed out the full skirt of her blue merino with the other, and then they moved slowly toward the door.

Brad's brown eyes lit up when he saw Annamarie.

"Oh, hullo, Annie! How's my girl?" he called to her as he piloted the girl to the door of the inn. Then he paused.

Annamarie didn't answer immediately, but stared at the slender figure that reminded her strangely of an icicle.

"You still waiting for me?" Brad added with a teasing grin as he paused with his hand holding the tall girl's elbow. "I want you to meet Linda Corling. Linda attended Mrs. Driscoll's Academy near the college and we met frequently. I hope you'll be friends. Her folks are also passengers. They were friends of my father years ago. Linda, this is Annamarie Tate and over there's Emmy Lou Hanks."

Annamarie tried to murmur words of greeting but the words stuck in her throat.

"You're not tongue-tied, are you, Annie?" Brad went on. "That isn't like you. She'll be a great addition to our crowd. Those are her parents just stepping from the stage. Linda's father is a lawyer." He pointed to an elaborately-dressed couple who seemed to ooze prestige.

Annamarie stood stiffly and swallowed hard. Linda still hadn't acknowledged Annamarie's presence as she gazed around at her new surroundings. *She seems stand-offish and a bit haughty,* Annamarie thought, *but she's very beautiful with the whitest skin I've ever seen. No wonder Brad's fallen for her . . .*

"Come on, Annie," Brad tucked his hand

under Annamarie's dimpled chin. "Don't be stuffy. Linda needs a friend. I told her about you, and I expect you to be that friend."

"I . . . of course, I'll be her f-friend," Annamarie gulped. "She . . . we . . . I'm just overwhelmed, I guess. I didn't expect —" she paused awkwardly.

Inwardly she felt uneasy. It was hard to know what to make of this — request.

Linda bowed slightly and murmured a few polite words in a husky voice, then followed her parents into the tavern. Annamarie's gaze followed the tall, beautiful girl's back, then she turned to face Brad, her gaze troubled. With a stiff smile tacked on her lips, she said, "I guess she's tired from the long ride."

"I'm sure she is. The Corlings will stay at Hays House until they've built a suitable place to live. I've told them all about Council Grove and what a great place it is. They're anxious to get settled.

"So . . . are services still held at the Brown Jug?" he asked with an impish grin. "Or are any new churches springing up?"

His eager boyishness was as warm and spontaneous as Annamarie remembered, and she nodded.

"Oh, yes. But you'd better explain to your . . . friend that the Brown Jug has nothing to do with what you normally find in a jug but that it's just what the schoolhouse has always been called. And yes, the Methodists are planning to build a church as soon as they raise enough funds."

"It's a good thing we've been able to hold services in that little brown schoolhouse all these years, not to mention using it as a city hall, concert and lecture hall," Brad commented.

Emmy Lou laughed as Annamarie continued, "Temperance meetings, chautauquas, lyceums, elections. I guess the Brown Jug's used for anything and everything where people need to meet."

"And there's a new schoolhouse, I hear?" He folded his arms across his broad chest.

"Yes, the two districts have finally built a graded school."

"And the Kaws? What of them?"

"The old Mission's no longer used for an Indian school, you know, but churches on the east side of town are holding services there now," Annamarie said. "My Indian friend, Po-a-be, has been going to school to learn English."

"Po-a-be?"

"It means 'little blue flower.' She lives on the reservation. She's become a special friend," Annamarie said, moving away. *Let*

Brad make the next move, she thought. *If he wants to see more of me, he'll have to ask to take me to prayer meeting tonight like he used to.*

He half-started for the tavern doorway, then turned. "Prayer meeting still on Wednesday night?"

She nodded and began to move down the street with Emmy Lou at her side. He hurried after her and touched her arm.

"Annie, it's been a long time since we sang together and, of course, you'll join me. Shall we plan to sing 'Oh, for a Closer Walk with God' as we did the Sunday before I left?" he asked with a quiet eagerness. "Like old times?"

Annamarie hesitated, "How about your friend . . . Linda? Will she be joining us?"

"Not tonight. Maybe later. She's tired from the long ride as you suspected. Just you and me — and the old crowd."

She turned away with a puzzled frown. She couldn't understand Brad's attitude. *Does he want me to go with him — only because Linda won't be there? It doesn't make sense.* With a quick nod, she and Emmy Lou hurried down the wooden walk as she called out over her shoulder, "Just you and me, Brad. I'll meet you at church."

CHAPTER 2

Annamarie pulled on her spotless white delaine with its white ruching around the neckline, then scrutinized her appearance in the mirror. She set her broad-brimmed black hat back upon her chestnut hair. *I won't need a hat this evening,* she thought, and took it off. She wrapped a knitted shawl around her shoulders for warmth during the cool fall evening. "I'll never be tall and graceful like Linda," she told herself as she bustled out of her bedroom toward the front door.

She hurried down the street just as twilight purpled the western sky. Already the vivid orange streaks had faded and the first stars winked in the early evening. A thin tendril of smoke licked up from the draw, probably from some camper cooking supper. Out of the south the cool autumn breezes had wafted from the hills; to the west the prairies dipped toward the draw. To the north it was prairie and more prairie.

Swinging her small lantern into an arc of light, she sped up the western slope of Belfry Hill. The small brown schoolhouse built from native timber sat prim and comfortable around the corner. It was unpainted and weatherbeaten, and had served as a schoolhouse when it was first built in 1858. Early pastors had served as teachers, and also preached in the little building on Sundays.

She remembered her school days there with happy memories: boys in homespun and high-top boots, girls in checkered aprons, their long braids tied back with a bit of string or a scrap of bright ribbon. Annamarie could still see the thumb-marked spellers, the initial-scarred desks, the old noisy slates and she smiled, remembering. Elwood Sharp and Kit Stenger were best known for their pranks but Jim Stenger was a model boy, known for not telling tales.

She was grateful that the rugged little building was shared by all faiths on Sundays. And of course, Wednesday night was always prayer meeting for everyone. Pastor Nash had served as well as director of the singing school. She was sure that in time each congregation would build its own church.

She stood near the schoolhouse looking for Brad's tall muscular figure. When he saw her he hurried up the hill.

"I should've picked you up, but you rushed away so fast this afternoon so I thought I'd better wait for you here," he said, taking her arm and leading her inside the small brown building. Kerosene lamps already glimmered in wall sconces and flickered eerily against the dark-painted walls.

"So good to finally see Brad in town," Ed Keitch said, jovially thumping Brad's broad shoulders.

"I guess we'll be favored by the unflappable duet between Annamarie and Brad," Dave Griggs bantered. "As usual."

"Her 'n Brad Bennett's just made for each other." Annamarie overheard Uncle Jimmy Watson's booming voice as she and Brad came in, and she blushed.

Pastor Nash beamed as they slipped into their seats near the front of the building. After the opening prayer, he announced quietly, "I shall ask Brother Brad and Sister Annamarie to sing number 329: 'Oh, for a Closer Walk with God.' They've sung it often before. No one can sing it with such meaning."

Brad took her elbow and led her to the front. He was right. They had sung together often before each of them had gone away, and when they stood side by side it was as if everyone knew their thoughts. For years they had used the same hymnal without embarrassment. But tonight she was wondering how Brad felt about it or if he was thinking about the tall slim blond. Their voices blended in harmony,

> *"Oh, for a closer walk with God,*
> *The calm and heavenly frame . . ."*

Annamarie was caught up in the beauty of the melody, the words that soothed and strengthened her. How she'd needed God these past years! Yes, it was good to have Brad back in town, and she thanked Him for bringing him home safely. Except . . .

The prayer meeting closed with prayers of thanksgiving and praise for Brad's return. Pastor Nash welcomed Brad back to Council Grove, and he smiled benignly on the group of young people who clustered near the doorway in the dim lantern light after the service.

"Linda would've loved our singing," Brad commented to Annamarie on the porch.

"Brad, we want to give you a 'welcome back' party. How about tomorrow night here in the Jug?" the pastor said. "We hear you brought a newcomer to Council Grove. Will she come, too?"

Annamarie shot a quick glance at Brad, and bit back a twinge of envy.

"Of course," Brad said with his usual eagerness. "Linda Corling needs to join our crowd of young folks. Annie here has already promised to be her friend. We all need to make her feel at home. Right, Annie?"

She stumbled a bit as she started down the porch steps. "Why, . . . y-yes," she faltered. "Sh-she needs us all, of course."

"That's my Annie," Brad said, grabbing her lantern as he took her arm. "It's time I see you home, my pretty maid. If you don't mind I'll walk you down to the house."

If she didn't mind! Hadn't he walked her home many times in the past? Hadn't she looked forward to his return for weeks? But had he changed? It seemed he had. He was still the dear, lovable Brad Bennett, with the gentle smile and the happy glow in his brown eyes.

His homecoming wasn't at all like Annamarie had hoped it would be because of Linda Corling's arrival. Linda seemed like such an alien here in this frontier town. She seemed so aloof. Yet she couldn't forget that Brad had expected Annamarie to share him with Linda, whom he obviously wanted to "show off." Maybe the welcome party would help them all to mingle. Still Annamarie felt uneasy. *Has Brad fallen in love with this slim blonde, and that's why he wants her to be popular?* she wondered. Tonight she'd had Brad mostly to herself, and their duet had seemed like old times. Almost . . .

The "welcome home" party was a huge success filled with bubbling laughter, happy party games and lots of gay camaraderie as the boys ribbed Brad about his college education.

Someone had fixed up a crown of fake dollar bills and set it rakishly on Brad's head. "FOR THE BANKER" it said. The crowd went into gales of laughter as they pranced around him.

Even Linda seemed to thaw a bit as she laughed with them. She stuck to Brad's side for the rest of the evening while Annamarie stood on the fringes, almost as an onlooker. Once she'd been with Brad, but now she turned over the privilege to Linda Corling. "I'm trying to be nice to her as he asked me to, but she seems more interested in *his* friendship than mine," she told Emmy Lou with a grimace. Later on, Brad tried to show her the same attention as before — except Linda was never far away.

Annamarie returned home that evening feeling disappointed about how her relationship with Brad seemed to be sliding backward instead of forward. She didn't see much of Brad as the weeks wore into November. The usual bustle of activity continued with Brad and some of the other young men chasing horse thieves and helping to move the stage line to Junction City, although the Santa Fe wagon trains still clattered into town for some time. The work that was involved took a lot of his time that month.

When the Methodists held their fundraiser at the Brown Jug, Brad asked Annamarie to go with him. He seemed like his happy, warm, spontaneous self, and she dressed carefully in her bright yellow merino with its lacy collar and full ruffled skirt. She wondered if Linda would decide to go without Brad.

"You look as pretty as a primrose," Emmy Lou told Annamarie as the two girls stood before the mirror in Annamarie's bedroom. "Now if only Linda Corling will have the decency to stay away, maybe Brad will pick this little flower!"

The two girls laughed. After all, Linda seldom attended their gatherings unless Brad took her. But did Brad feel obligated to ask Annamarie, especially if Linda didn't want to go? *Was I his second choice?* she wondered.

That evening Brad arrived promptly to walk Annamarie and Emmy Lou to the fundraiser. When they arrived Linda was already there, whirling around gaily, looking very smooth in a dark red wool dress that set off her blond beauty exquisitely. They were in the middle of "Skip to My Lou," and she attached herself to Brad the minute he and his two companions came in.

"Oh, Brad," she cooed, "I wondered if you'd come or you'd have to work at your ol' bank. Is it going well?"

"Never better. But then, Council Grove's booming. I'm glad to know your parents are building a new home. This will be an added attraction for our town."

The familiar stab of envy shot through Annamarie again at his words, and she prayed quietly, *Lord, please don't let me be jealous of Brad's interest in her. After all, she is a newcomer and needs Brad, too . . .*

As he pushed his way through the crowd with two plates of food, he handed one to Linda and one to Emmy Lou. With a sly grin he turned to Annamarie.

"Annie, I'll get ours now. Still like apple cider? Or is it coffee?"

She smiled coyly. "No, I haven't taken up drinking coffee yet. Who can afford to buy it at today's prices? I'll have the cider, thank you."

The fundraiser seemed to go well, and Annamarie almost felt at ease with Linda. After all, Brad seemed to treat both girls alike, with his usual gallantry. And he *had* brought her.

Fall slipped quietly into winter and the air grew chill. Parties and activities mushroomed all over town. Among the newcomers were the Hammond girls, the Dillon girls, the Matthews sisters, escorted by the Stenger boys and George Huffaker. Quilting bees kept Annamarie and Emmy Lou jumping from home to home during the following weeks.

One cold gray afternoon Annamarie stopped by the newly finished Corling house to see Linda. The beautiful house boasted green shutters and a doorbell. As she rang the doorbell, she had second thoughts about her impulse to drop by this way.

"Hello, Mrs. Corling. I'm Annamarie Tate, a fr-friend of Linda's. Is sh-she home this afternoon?"

"No, but do come in for a moment to warm yourself, Annamarie. You must be freezing out there." Annamarie hesitated, but a blast of cold wind nudged her over the doorstep. As Annamarie stepped inside, Mrs. Corling continued, "No, she's gone out for a few hours, but you're welcome to stay and have some coffee if you'd like."

Annamarie felt rather awkward about the thought of sitting there sipping coffee when

Linda returned home so she declined the invitation.

"I'll tell her you stopped by then," Mrs. Corling replied with a stiff smile as she opened the door for Annamarie's departure.

Annamarie had noticed the ingrain carpet and a shiny new pump organ in the corner. Kerosene lamps with floral designs in muted shades graced every small table in the spacious parlor. Annamarie couldn't resist a twinge of envy at the lush new house. *Does Brad visit here often?* she wondered. If he did, he never mentioned it. She remembered Mrs. Corling had not said where Linda was for "a few hours," and she hurried home before it got dark.

In her spare time, Annamarie worked on her needlework — a Bible verse with

CASTING ALL YOUR CARE UPON HIM; FOR HE CARETH FOR YOU (1 Peter 5:7)

stitched neatly in brightly colored yarn. She hung it on the shabby Tate parlor wall. At least she'd do her part in making their simple two-story home more cheery. Through her efforts in the three upstairs bedrooms, there were new quilts on the beds and embroidered scarves on the bureaus.

From her upstairs bedroom window she

34

could look out to the north and see the craggy cliff rising up from Belfry Hill. In one of the crevices was tucked the mysterious Hermit's Cave. Here, for a time, lived the "hermit priest of the Santa Fe Trail," as he was called. He was said to be a lonely Italian man who had lived for some months in the cave in the cliff until one day he vanished. No one had seen him since.

The cave, with its crevices and clefts, became "Cupid's post office" where the young people from town hid their love notes to each other. Before Brad had left for the East, he and Annamarie had occasionally hidden their letters in one tiny nook in a special cleft. But since he had come back he hadn't mentioned it. She wondered if he'd forgotten it.

Annamarie stood at the window and stared at the fading winter sunset. The sun had dropped behind the prairies far across the valley and touched the draw with purple. She recalled the days when Brad had walked her home and they had paused by the cave. Their many walks to the draw, sometimes on horseback, had been special times.

"Annie," he had said softly one day, "let's never forget this place — where we can hide our special messages to each other. If you ever want to tell me something, hide your letter in that cleft right above the cave opening. Then I'll know where to look."

Shortly afterward he had gone away to Ohio and she had left for Illinois. But since his return to Kansas, he hadn't once mentioned the draw or the cave. It was as though he had forgotten their trysting places.

After the new year of 1868 was ushered in with its usual round of parties, noise and games, news came that General Custer was camping near Council Grove. This famous general had caused quite a controversy according to the news Annamarie's father had brought home one evening.

"My, what a stir that's created," Joseph Tate remarked when he came home from the blacksmith shop. He hung his smoke-stained gray fedora behind the door. "His camp's located north of the Sampletown bridge. Rumors have it that he wants to buy a farm from the Kaw Indians. To have such a celebrity here —"

"Well, he isn't the only famous person to visit here," Sara Tate added tartly as she brought the chicken to the table. "It's also been rumored that Susan B. Anthony is coming to the Brown Jug to lecture on women's suffrage! We need to close the saloons. It's tempting the Indians to spend their allotment on drink."

"Well, women weren't meant to vote, if

that's what she's after. I think I can find that in the Bible someplace!" Joseph Tate snorted.

The conversation that had quickly turned sour over women's suffrage fell into silence as the meal was served by Mrs. Tate and her younger daughter, Susan. Annamarie's brooding over Brad seemed to add to the heavy mood.

Brad was busy at the bank and Annamarie saw little of him during the cold, brittle months — except in church. Usually Linda Corling, looking more like a fragile icicle than ever, managed to slip in by Brad's side. She seemed to listen intently to Pastor Nash's message.

Linda had never acknowledged that her mother had told her about Annamarie's visit. Annamarie wondered if Linda had been with Brad that day so she decided not to mention it. She assumed that Linda wasn't interested in pursuing another visit from her.

"The Lord alone knows what is in Brad's heart," Annamarie told herself. "But if he's changed his mind about me, surely he'll tell me soon."

The snow fell heavily as winter progressed and shut them in for days at a time. Annamarie scarcely saw anyone from her crowd of friends during the remainder of the winter, with the exception of Po-a-be, who dropped by fairly often. March's latest snowfall had left the streets raw and muddy as the feeble sunlight needled through the thin, high clouds. Spring couldn't arrive too soon for Council Grove that year.

A few weeks later the town was agog with the news of the escape of Sarah Jane Lester from the Indians. Po-a-be had told Annamarie how Sarah Jane had been captured by the Cheyennes and taken to southeastern Kansas, where her parents had been killed. Apparently, she had made several attempts to get away and was finally able to steal a pony from them and ride down the Santa Fe Trail.

This news was the main topic of conversation at Emmy Lou's birthday party.

"I would hate to be in the hands of the Cheyennes," Po-a-be said.

"The horror stories she's told," Linda shuddered as she stared at Po-a-be. "They make you want to hop the next stage back to civilization!"

I almost wish you would, Annamarie thought. *And leave Brad behind.* Then she scolded herself stoutly. *I must be loving and forgiving, not catty.* But why was it so hard?

CHAPTER 3

Joseph Tate left for Topeka on a business trip the first week in April, leaving Annamarie and Susan to help their mother with the spring work in the garden.

Every evening they gathered near the stove to catch the last rays of warmth as they did their sewing. Annamarie finished hemming the final pair of pantaloons.

"I don't know how you can stand making these fancy undergarments," Susan grouched, throwing down her needle and thread. "I wish we didn't have to be so stylish! Why can't we be like Po-a-be, and wear simple cambric dresses without the folderol of worrying about what to wear underneath?"

Annamarie laughed. "Wait 'til you're fourteen, Susan. You'll want to wear fancy doodads, too."

"Well, I'm glad I'm only twelve, and don't have to worry about such things."

A knock sounded on the side door, and at Annamarie's call, Po-a-be let herself in like a quiet shadow and sat down on the chair next to Annamarie. A bright orange shawl covered her thin shoulders, and her dark eyes glittered as she flipped one black braid down her neck.

"You making such pretty things," she said, picking up one finished undergarment. "You think Linda wear these things?"

"That's why Annamarie makes hers so fancy with lacy trim," Susan snorted. "I just told her that I wish we'd wear garments like you Indians do."

Po-a-be's smile lit up her dark face. "Sometimes I like pretties, too. But that is not important today. I bring news — bad news.

"I hear a runner from Cheyenne talk to Running Elk. He say Kaws should be angry with town people. Indian agent won't let Kaws use allotment money for whiskey. You tell Brad there could be a fight with white people."

"Surely the Kaws wouldn't fight us, would they? They've been our friends since 1859, after that last skirmish."

"Some Kaws would like the firewater, and say people in the town try to keep them away from tavern," Po-a-be said quietly. She went to the window and looked out.

"Do you really think they'd rise up against us? It's hard to believe," Annamarie gulped.

Po-a-be turned away from the window, her

dark eyes brooding. "Tell Brad, 'Be careful.' Running Elk, he good friend with Brad. He would listen to Brad." She turned to the door. "Brad like you, Annamarie. He will listen to what you say." Then she slid out of the door and was gone.

Brad liked her? Annamarie's face was pensive. Sometimes she wondered about that — since Linda Corling had come to town. But if this was true and the Kaws were unhappy about the way the Indian agent was handling things, the people in town should know. Maybe Brad could talk sense to Running Elk.

Laying down her sewing, she went to look for her mother. She found her in the bedroom, seated on the walnut bed with its calico valance around the top and a tester of the same flowered material on the bottom. A Bible lay open on her lap. "Mother —" Annamarie began.

Sara Tate looked up. "Anything wrong, daughter? You look disturbed."

"Po-a-be was here. Sh-she insists that Running Elk has been in touch with a runner from the Cheyenne to urge the Kaws to attack the town. But —"

"We have friends among the Kaws, you know. I doubt very much that they'd do anything foolish."

"Still, Po-a-be usually knows what she's talking about. She says I should tell Brad to warn the city fathers."

Her mother paged through the Bible. "We have our hope in the Lord. Right here in Psalm 56:3 it says, 'What time I am afraid I will trust in thee.' And in Isaiah 25:1 it says, 'O LORD, thou art my God; I will exalt thee, I will praise thy name; for thou hast done wonderful things; thy counsels of old are faithfulness and truth.' Let's keep trusting Him. Still, if you feel easier telling Brad, then go ahead."

"Thank you, Mother. It's that Po-a-be's my friend, too, and she wouldn't tell me this if she weren't concerned." She turned to go back to the kitchen.

Picking up her shawl from the hook behind the door in the little alcove, she let herself out the door. *I'll feel awfully foolish if this is silly talk,* she thought. *But somehow I think I'd better do this.*

As she sped up the street toward the bank, a soft April breeze blew whiffs of Bouncing Bets that lay crushed in the draw. Their sweetness wafted over the valley in massive waves.

She heard pounding footsteps as Sally Brown came running toward her with a drab gray slat bonnet pushed from her thin, sunburned face and her scrawny yellow braids flapping in the wind.

"Annamarie! Where are you . . . headed so fast?" she panted.

Annamarie stopped. "Downtown. I need to talk to Brad at the bank."

"Oh him! I just saw him and that tall skinny blond hiking up the cliff path. If I was you, I'd hog-tie him fast. That girl's sure got her claws in him, and he don't seem to know what she's doing!"

"Well," Annamarie gulped. "Of course, I don't own Brad. He doesn't belong to me any more than he does to her. I-I'm s'posed to be her friend, although she . . . she scarcely gives me the time of day."

"Well, go on! Go on after them. If you have a message for him, you'd better catch him before she ties him up. After all, you knew him first!"

With a sudden burst of vigor Annamarie turned and scrambled up the cliff path. She didn't have time to conjecture what Brad and Linda might have to say to each other that was so important they had to go up to the cliff. She had just seen them disappear around the bend by the cave, and she hurried faster, her shoes kicking up whiffs of gravel and dirt as she ran. She was about ready to call out to Brad when she saw — them.

Linda was in his arms, sobbing bitter tears against his chest. His arms were around her and he stroked her soft hair, gently murmuring.

"There, there, Linda. You know you'll always have me. Don't worry about a thing!"

A pang of anguish knifed through Annamarie and she turned away, heartsick. So it was true. Brad loved Linda. Obviously he didn't have the courage to tell Annamarie or figured it wasn't her business.

She whirled away and fled down the path, heading back down the trail, stones and rocks clattering as she ran. Tears stung her eyes and coursed down her pink cheeks. This was the end of her dreams of a future with Brad Bennett. She was sure of it.

CHAPTER 4

Oh, Brad, Brad. . . . The cry was deep within her. *I thought I mattered. Somehow I had always felt I could count on your love, your friendship. But now I know I was a trifle, and you toyed with my affections. When you asked me to wait for you, it was all a game with you. But if that's what you want, I won't stand in your way.* Her pain was so sharp that she didn't know how she could ever stand it.

"I should've stayed in Illinois with Grandma and Grandpa Lipscombe," she murmured in agony. "One reason I came back was because I knew Brad would be home. After all, he'd asked me to wait . . . and I loved him. But I didn't know Linda would steal his heart."

She drew a deep ragged sigh as she walked slowly down the street toward home.

"How will I ever face life again?" she mumbled aloud with a half-sob. "I know what I must do. I'll write him a letter and leave it in our secret 'post office.' I'll tell him —" What would she tell him? That she *couldn't* see him, knowing he loved another?

As she turned onto Pine Street, she knew she would have to tell her mother something. *Lord, please be my strength, my shield!*

She opened the kitchen door and let herself in quietly. The house was quiet except for the gentle thumping of the lid on a kettle of beef stew simmering on the stove. Then from the bedroom she heard the sound of weeping and she slipped into her parents' bedchamber. Her mother lay huddled in a heap on the bed, her shoulders heaving with great sobs. What was wrong? Mother had always been so strong.

"Mother?" she spoke softly, and her mother's sobs ceased for a moment as she sat up, her care-worn face red and swollen with tears.

"Oh, Annamarie, I . . . it's so hard."

"What's so hard, Mother?"

Blowing her nose with a small soggy handkerchief, Sara Tate threw out her arms.

"They . . . they came half an hour ago to tell me. Your father's been . . . killed. He . . . he was on his way home from Topeka when apparently Blackbird was spooked and he threw your father to the ground on the trail from Clear Ridge. That's where he was found. His skull fractured . . . bones broken —"

"Who found him?" Annamarie shot back.

Shock and disbelief crushed her senses. This couldn't have happened! Her strong, stalwart father —

"A . . . freighter brought the message to town. He told the marshal who came here."

"But how did they know it was Joseph Tate?" Annamarie whispered. "They could've made a mistake . . . someone else —"

Her mother shook her held fiercely. "No. There was no mistake. See that?" she pointed to the soft, gray fedora sitting on the dresser. "That's your father's hat. It's one he's worn for years."

Annamarie picked up the worn fedora and turned it over carefully. Sweat-stained, grimy with smoke from the forge in his shop — there was no mistake.

"Where is his body?" Annamarie asked hoarsely.

"They're bringing it here. I sent Susan to tell Pastor Nash. But oh, Annamarie, I never dreamed your father wouldn't come back when he left!" She broke into sobs again.

Annamarie held her mother gently and stroked the shaking shoulders. Why had their father been taken from them so suddenly? *Oh, dear Lord, why have You allowed these . . . these sorrows to come upon us? Brad lost to me and now Father gone.* She choked back the sobs that threatened to overwhelm her.

Susan was weeping when she came into the house with the pastor, her freckled face streaked with tears. Annamarie heard them talking in the kitchen. *I must be strong for Susan and Mother, Lord.*

Suddenly Sara Tate took a deep breath, dried her eyes, got up and went into the kitchen. She poured a drink of water for Pastor Nash, who waited by the table. His lined face looked kind and compassionate, his gray hair tousled from the wind.

He took Mrs. Tate's hand and pressed it warmly. "Please, if there's anything I can do —"

"I'm grateful you've come and I know you must help plan the burial services. I . . . the girls need me, and I'll be all right in a moment." She sighed heavily.

Pastor Nash sat down at the table and sipped the water slowly. "I'm sure you will. Remember, in Proverbs it says to 'Trust in the Lord with all your heart, and lean not to your own understanding,' even if it's hard to understand now. Are you ready to plan the services?"

"Yes," her mother replied softly.

Annamarie never knew how she made it through the grueling hours that followed. Throughout the afternoon friends and neighbors stopped by with kettles of soup, casseroles and pies still warm from the oven. *How we'll ever feel like eating again is a mystery,* Annamarie told herself. But not to have to think of fixing food was a relief.

Amazing as it seemed, guests with their condolences and baskets of food continued to arrive until Annamarie despaired of knowing where to put all the food. Her mother seemed to be handling the situation with newfound strength. In all the preoccupation of planning her father's funeral and acknowledging the friends who came by, Annamarie had all but forgotten Po-a-be's message until now.

She was so overwhelmed by her father's death that everything else seemed unreal, unimportant. She couldn't relay the message to anyone now and especially not to Brad. *I can't deal with it all now! Please help me!* she prayed.

During the days following her father's death, Annamarie felt numb and more dead than alive. It seemed she had buried Brad as well as her father. To her surprise Brad came by one evening, his dear face lined and grim. He took Annamarie's hands in his and squeezed them gently.

"I'm so sorry, Annie. The whole town's shaken up with this tragic news. If there's anything I can do —"

She withdrew her hands quickly and turned away. "There's nothing anyone can do except pray for the Lord to give us grace and strength." She bowed her head to hide the tears that spilled from her eyes.

"You know I'll do that. Please feel free to share your feelings with me. You know I've always cared."

She jerked up her head. "Have you, Brad? I —" She swallowed the lump in her throat. "Right now, please leave me alone! I must be strong — for my mother and sister." Abruptly she whirled around and walked away.

Emmy Lou's quiet presence was a soothing balm. Her friend came often during the following days to help with little jobs like hoeing the garden and helping with laundry, or walking to Greenwood Cemetery with her. The clodded mound with the wilted prairie blossoms was like an ugly wart on the face of a peaceful meadow. The sight of it made her realize that her father would never again stir the coals of his forge in the blacksmith shop nor strike his hot iron on the anvil.

I don't know how I could've managed without my best friend, she told herself.

One early morning a week later Annamarie made her way pensively toward town on an errand for her mother. The air was sweet and cool and a heavy mist hung in the air.

"How we'll manage without his income I don't know," Sara Tate had said that morning. "He felt the need to go to Topeka to arrange for a government post for his brother, your Uncle Tom, so he could move to Kansas, you know. But now we'll never know how the interview went, I fear."

"Mother," Annamarie tried to be reassuring, "somehow there's got to be a way for us."

"Yes, I was thinking that we have some extra upstairs rooms. There's our huge garden plot and orchard in the back, which yields abundant fruits and vegetables. We could turn the two large rooms upstairs over to boarders if you and Susan shared the small bedroom."

"If there was only something I could do to help Mother," Annamarie mused aloud as she recalled the conversation with her mother an hour earlier. "This will be hard on Susan. She's forced to grow up faster than normal."

Reaching Main Street she turned into the store for the cornmeal her mother had asked her to bring. Just then she heard someone behind her. Turning around, she saw Po-a-be's slight figure and her gentle face.

"Oh, my friend," the Indian girl spoke in her soft voice, "I feel so sad your father has gone on his last great hunt. How is it going with you?"

Annamarie smiled wanly. "Somehow we will make it. We'll take in boarders who'll pay for food and lodging. Our God will help us, but we must do all we can, too."

"You give Brad my message?" Po-a-be spoke anxiously. "About the Cheyenne?"

"The message!" Annamarie gasped. In the agony of grief of seeing Brad with Linda and her father's death she had pushed it to the back of her mind. She only hoped it wasn't too late.

"Oh, Po-a-be . . . I'm truly sorry. When I came home and I received word of my father's death, I forgot everything else."

"But you did see Brad, did you not?"

Annamarie shook her head. "No, Po-a-be. I'd followed him up the cliff path then I saw him with Linda. I overheard —"

"What did you overhear?"

"Brad," Annamarie's lips quivered, "He . . . held Linda in his arms and . . . and said she'd always have him. I knew I couldn't talk to him then, so I hurried home. That's when my mother gave me the message about Father. After that —"

"I can see you must hurt so bad. Your

God will give you courage. But didn't he come to see you after he heard about your father?"

Annamarie was quiet. What should she say? "I — yes, he did. But I was so upset —" *I can't tell her that part of my upset was because of Linda,* she thought. "I didn't think to tell him. What's happened to the rumor about the fight?"

Po-a-be's dark eyes smoldered. "Running Elk knows more than he tells. But yes — the Cheyennes plan to come to the reservation soon. You will tell Brad?"

"I'll make sure he knows. I'm sorry I didn't do it sooner. But I will."

With a wave of her brown hand, Po-a-be spun around and sped down the trail.

Annamarie watched her go. This time she'd do as she'd promised. She'd find Brad and give him the message.

Slowly she started down the street toward the bank. *If only I didn't have to face him,* she mused. *I'll never forget the scene of Linda in Brad's arms.*

Just then stocky Dave Griggs and tall, lanky Ed Keitch barreled out of the hardware store, laughing and joking as usual. They stopped short when they saw her.

"Well, if it isn't the town belle — and we don't mean the alarm bell," Ed joshed.

"What's new, that you've traded your fresh Kansas look for that poker face?"

"Oh," Annamarie paused. Why not tell them to give Brad the message? "I might as well tell you. I just met Po-a-be who gave me some news."

"What news?" Dave flipped back his cap. "That the Methodists were determined to get the first organ for church service but the Presbyterians voted it in since Linda's rich father is expected to donate it? And why would that give you such a sober face? Are you playing a joke on us?"

"No, no. It's much more serious than that. She says — in fact, she told me over a week ago — that the Cheyenne are heading toward Council Grove. They want the Kaws to attack the town for not allowing them to buy whiskey with their allotment."

"Not buy whiskey! Now Susan B. Anthony would want it that way!" Ed hooted with laughter. "But that's absolutely absurd. I don't believe it."

"Neither do I," Dave snorted. "The Kaws have always been peaceful and we've had little trouble with them in the past. Why should they want to attack us now?"

Annamarie took off her blue sunbonnet and toyed with the ties. "Po-a-be insists Running Elk has been in touch with them.

She wanted me to tell Brad, but then my father was killed and I couldn't think straight. So I forgot to tell anyone. I wondered if the two of you would give Brad the message."

"Why not tell him yourself? Don't tell me you don't need a good excuse to talk to Bradford Bennett!" Ed scoffed.

Annamarie carefully smoothed her dark hair and set the bonnet back on her head. "Well, you know, since Linda's come to town, it's . . . it's been hard to . . . to catch him alone."

"So that's the catch. I see what you mean. Brad hasn't paid much attention to you, has he? Well, he's got more than bankin' on his mind these days. That tall blond, you know. But we'll see that he gets the message. Him and the marshall both. Don't you worry."

Annamarie watched them go. Were there some implications in Ed's response about Brad and Linda? She didn't know. But she knew they'd tell him what Po-a-be had said.

She hurried up the street to check the price of bacon. These days it was hard to know what they could afford and what they couldn't. *If only there was some way I could help Mother out by helping earn a living,* she thought. *But single girls don't work in the public market place.*

Just as she turned up Pine Street she heard the sound of running footsteps behind her. As she turned, she saw Brad's bareheaded figure flying to catch up with her, and she paused.

"Annie! Annie!" he panted. "Ed and Dave practically kidnapped me from the bank and muttered some stupid message about the Cheyennes' plan to make the Kaws attack the town. Now tell me exactly what Po-a-be said."

She moistened her dry lips. Brad looked as dear as ever, and she had to choose her words carefully. She couldn't mention seeing him with Linda.

"That's what she told me over a week ago. She says Running Elk has been in touch with the Cheyennes. They're up to no good, from what she says."

"But Running Elk would never — Annie Tate, why didn't you tell me sooner?"

"I tried," she began as she remembered the unforgettable scene of Brad and Linda on the cliff path. "After I got the message about my father, I forgot everything else. Then when I met Dave and Ed just now —"

"But why did you send them to tell me, instead of coming yourself? You and I have always been friends. We've shared so many things. I can't understand why you're avoiding me, Annie!"

She shook her head. What could she say? That she was afraid she'd start crying when she talked to him? And why hadn't he told her about himself and Linda? She turned and walked away before the tears welling up in her eyes began to spill down her cheeks.

CHAPTER 5

May Day party plans were the talk of the town. It was an annual event and an excuse for the community to spend a day in merry-making and frolic.

Annamarie wasn't surprised when the town's choice for May Queen was Linda Corling. No one was as self-assured, graceful and appealing as the tall, slim blond.

"You going to be one of the attendants?" Emmy Lou asked her as the two girls hung the last batch of clothes on the line. The spicy sent of wild roses wafted thick and sweet through the late spring air, mingling with a touch of honeysuckle that clung to the back yard gate.

Annamarie finished hanging up her faded blue percale, its full skirt billowing in the stiff breeze. "Not if I can help it. I know Brad will be one of the key people at the festivities, being a member of the business community sponsoring the May Day festival. I'd always thought . . ." She paused, snapping the last clothespin to the line.

"You always thought you had a special

place in Brad's life," Emmy Lou cut in. "I could just shake him until his teeth fall out. What he sees in that . . . that icicle, and for the way he ignores you, Annamarie, it doesn't seem fair that an outsider like her should have the part of the May Queen! You're as pretty as she is — prettier, if you ask me. Why did she have to prance into town as if she owned it — and Brad, too? It's more than I can figure out!"

"Linda Corling has as much right to live here as anyone," Annamarie said quickly, picking up the empty wicker basket and starting for the house.

"Oh, I don't see how you can be so . . . so self-sacrificing and forgiving when it comes to her! And to let her get away with stealing Brad right from under your nose!"

Annamarie held the kitchen door open. "That was Brad's choice, not mine. At least, he and I still sing together in church most Sundays. It's something Linda doesn't seem to do."

"Sing!" Emmy Lou laughed. "Have you ever heard her sing? She screeches like a hawk."

"Oh, it's not that bad. But she has that lost, appealing look about her that seems to grab people."

She set the basket in the lean-to and took

a mixing bowl from the pantry shelf.

"Well, being the daughter of one of Council Grove's richest citizens has its advantages," Emmy Lou said with a sigh.

"As long as Brad asks me to sing with him on Sundays I can't fail him. I'm doing it for the Lord, not for the glory," Annamarie said, her eyes moist as she poured flour into the bowl and broke a few eggs into it. "I'd better get the muffins into the oven if we're ever to get out to the Maypole ceremonies on time. It was good of you to help, Emmy Lou. I trust the clothes will be dry by two o'clock. You'll meet me there?"

"Of course. Now I'd better rush home." She dashed off and slammed the back door as she left.

The next hour passed quickly. Already Mrs. Tate's one boarder, the editor of the *Council Grove Advertiser*, Will Johnson, kept her mother busy planning meals. The son of a veteran Kansas newspaperman, Mr. Johnson was a mild-mannered little man who kept hours that were often sporadic because of his irregular work at the newspaper office.

Fortunately today he had made sure of his noon meal before rushing out to the middle of town with his note pad. Annamarie swept the kitchen floor, then changed into her pale green delaine with its tiny white collar. She

60

knew the green clashed with her blue eyes, but she couldn't afford to be choosy, and the blue gingham was not ironed. It was hard enough to think of Linda Corling in a filmy pink cheesecloth gown being crowned Queen of May without worrying about what dress to wear.

Already the streets swarmed with people when she arrived — girls and women in hoop skirts and bustles, children romping around the Maypole to the music of a few squeaky fiddles and raucous cornets spilling out rusty tunes. Susan had left early to participate in the Maypole activities.

As Annamarie looked for Emmy Lou in the swirling crowds, she felt a sudden tug at her elbow. Turning, she saw Brad's merry grin.

"What's your big hurry, Annie? I hardly ever see you anymore. I'm sorry I can't be everywhere at once and escort you properly today, but I have an obligation to fulfill," he bantered.

She eyed him saucily. "To escort the Queen of May, no doubt. Of course, she —"

"They wanted one of the younger crowd to head the afternoon's events, you know, much to my dismay. For once I thought I'd have the pleasure of you hanging on my arm. But you can see it's not to be. Still, I think you've avoided me lately, Annie, my dear," he added wryly.

Annamarie squinted at the warm summer sky. Brad hadn't paid much attention to her for months. Now that Linda was "royalty" for the afternoon and he couldn't accompany her to the festivities, he pretended to be too occupied with other duties. She frowned.

"Uh, I've been . . . helping Mother since she opened the boarding house. And there's always gardening and cleaning —"

"Not every minute of the day, Annie Tate!" he cut in. "Tell me, you haven't been avoiding me on purpose, have you?"

"Well," she said awkwardly, looking down the street. "Look, I think they're waiting on you. It's time for the festivities to start."

Abruptly he hurried toward Uncle Jimmie Watson, who was the committee chairman.

The singing of pink-cheeked girls heralded the winding of the Maypole as the tall, graceful May queen stepped daintily to receive her tiara of red prairie lilies and wild blue iris. Linda Corling, looking like a delicate piece of pink-frosted cake, received generous applause as General MacMillan placed the crown on her fine-spun gold hair. *I could never have done it so gracefully*, Annamarie reminded herself.

The late afternoon shadows lay lightly on

the prairies like a phantom boat on a mystic sea as the crowd moved away from the maypole. To climax the fete, ice cream freezers appeared in the shade of a nearby elm. The clatter of bowls and spoons mingled with the eager clamor of merrymaking.

Suddenly Uncle Jimmie waved his arms. "I guess we'd better squelch the rumors around here," he boomed. "There's all this talk about the Kaws attackin' the town. If that ain't a bunch of foolishness —"

"I'm not so sure of that, Uncle Jimmie," Brad cut in tartly. "I've talked to Running Elk myself. He says —"

"Don't anybody believe it. We're used to rumors of Indian attacks and guerilla raids! You know that blamed well, Bennett," Horace Rawlins shouted hoarsely.

Brad placed his hands on his hips. "Running Elk tells me we'd better be prepared to defend ourselves. General Stover has promised to come to the reservation to help the Kaws, if they need it," he went on. "It's time to make plans, since we're all together here."

"Yeah. *If* it happens — but I'm not sayin' it will —" Jacob Barth said stoutly. "Someone's gotta be responsible for ringin' the alarm bell."

Annamarie knew the alarm bell had originally been molded for a church in Lawrence but when it had arrived with a crack, the church had refused it. Colonel Wood knew that Council Grove needed an alarm bell and brought it into town by ox team where it was erected on Belfry Hill. It was intended to warn people of Indian attacks and fires as well as call people to worship and children to school. And of course, ringing out the old year and welcoming the new. Now it could summon the people together if the Indians came.

After a low-voiced hasty discussion with a group of town leaders, Uncle Jimmie's booming voice rang out again. "Here's what we're gonna do. When the bell rings, wimmin and children is to go to Hebrank's Brewery basement while us menfolks arm ourselves and protect the town. Is that clear?"

There was a low murmur of voices as people took in what was said. Annamarie glanced around quickly. She knew her sister Susan had been in the group which had whirled around the Maypole, but she'd seen nothing of her mother. *I only hope this news won't shake her up,* she thought. Being a widow, Sara Tate took her responsibility of looking after her girls seriously. Then Annamarie saw her mother walking away, arm-in-arm with Susan, her face determined and confident.

"Isn't it awful!" Emmy Lou whispered, grabbing her arm. "When the Indians attack the town —"

"We don't know that," Annamarie said in a low voice.

"But Brad said he'd talked to Running Elk —"

"It's just that we must be prepared. The question is *if*, not when."

"Do you s'pose Brad will know beforehand? Then you'll let us know, won't you?"

Annamarie shook her head fiercely. "I have no idea how soon I'll know. Besides, even if Brad knows, why should it concern me?"

"But I saw you and Brad —"

"I'm not counting on anything with Brad anymore."

"I was sure I saw you two together two hours ago . . ."

"He was bemoaning the fact that he couldn't have me hanging onto his arm because he was one of the officials! Then he stalked off — since apparently he couldn't be with Linda. I still don't see why he has to have us both. But I'm getting tired of it."

Emmy Lou shrugged her shoulders and announced that she was going to walk home. They walked together until Annamarie turned down Pine Street. As she recalled the day's events, a sense of foreboding gripped her and she couldn't shake it off. The warm sun was slanting toward the horizon and the wide prairies lay in the shadows of a few clouds as May Day drew to a close.

CHAPTER 6

On June 3, 1868, the harsh insistent toll of the alarm bell shattered the quiet air. Annamarie looked up from her breakfast oatmeal and paused with her spoon in midair.

"Oh, Mother!" she gasped. "It's the . . . the Indian alarm! That's the cue for us to rush to Hebrank's Brewery!" She jumped up and grabbed the two loaves of bread from the table and stuffed them into a clean flour sack. "Come on. We'd better hurry! I'll take this food. We may be there awhile."

Susan looked at her, fear in her blue eyes. "Does this mean Indians are coming?" she cried.

Annamarie nodded. "Yes, I think so. Come. Let's go!" She grabbed Susan's arm and began to pull her toward the door. Her mother stopped to rummage in the hall closet.

"Mother! Aren't you coming?" she called impatiently.

"I want to pick up a few keepsakes — your father's Civil War momentos —"

"No! We don't have time for that!" She

shoved her sister and mother out the door and led the way down the hill toward the brewery. Just then she saw a runner waving his arms and shouting.

"The Cheyennes are coming! Run! Hurry out to the brewery basement!"

From all over town women and children were scrambling toward the building. The two-story tiled walls seemed like a bulwark against the enemy, and she pushed her mother and sister rudely through the heavy door.

"Go down the stairs," she ordered. "I'll come down as soon as I can."

She spied Emmy Lou, Sally Brown and a few others in one corner, kneeling in prayer. All over the dank room she heard women praying and she paused.

"But Annamarie," her mother called anxiously. "you said the basement —"

"I'll stay here and pray. Don't worry. Go on downstairs!"

As she joined her friends in their prayer corner, she glanced at one of the windows and caught sight of hordes of Cheyenne warriors, faces painted in lurid war colors, running down the street, and she shuddered.

"Oh, dear Lord," she cried aloud, "Please keep us safe!"

Just then Brad Bennett stormed through

the door. "They're not after us, they say!" he shouted. "They're after the Kaws!"

"But why are they after the Kaws?" a plaintive voice whimpered.

Brad shook his head. "I'm not sure. They say the Kaws have broken the Indian laws and deserve to be punished!" He motioned to some mothers and their children who had just straggled in, and waved them toward the basement. From everywhere in the room children cried and whined in fear. "Just keep out of sight, and I'm sure you'll be safe! Now I must talk to Running Elk." He hurried toward Annamarie. "You all right? Please take care!" His voice sounded urgent. "Annie, if anything happened to you —"

"I'll be all right." she said quietly. "But I haven't seen Linda. If I do, I'll look after her . . . if that's what you want."

He looked at her strangely. "Please do. She's always so fearful!" Then he whirled around toward the door and rushed out.

Mrs. Metzker stood in the doorway like a commanding general, trying to keep the Cheyennes from pushing their way inside. Emmy Lou and the other girls were still praying when Annamarie noticed Linda cowering in one corner, crying softly. She hurried toward her and placed one arm around the heaving shoulders.

"Don't cry! The Lord will protect us," she soothed, stroking the pale hair. "Please be calm."

The slim blond clung to her and whispered, "Oh, Annamarie — Where's Brad? Did he go to the reservation? Have you seen him?"

"Yes, he . . . he came in to check if we were all here. I told him I'd look after you."

"Did he ask about me?"

Annamarie hesitated. He hadn't asked about Linda. "He has a lot on his mind. I'm sure he meant to. Just calm down!"

She was aware of activity by the door and made her way cautiously toward Mrs. Metzker to find out what was happening.

The older woman's plump face looked grim but quite composed. She turned when Annamarie touched her arm.

"They want food and they want water. That's all. Otherwise I think they'll leave us alone," she replied as she went to the basement to dip more water from the well.

"I brought some bread," Annamarie said. "You can give it to them," she called out over her shoulder, picking up the two loaves from the corner where she had tossed the sack when she came in. To think Mother had spent hours baking these loaves from their meager supply of flour, only to pacify the Cheyennes! But lives were more important than food, even though Brad had reassured them the Indians were after the Kaws and wanted only food and water in town.

She felt a touch as Linda Corling's slim hand trembled on her arm. "What's happening? Why is Mrs. Metzker dipping all that water from the well?"

Annamarie let out a sigh. "That's all the Indians are after. I also gave them the bread I brought —"

"But if they want food, God knows what else they're after!" Linda sniffled, her face carved with fear.

"Please believe me, Linda," she said in an absurdly patient voice, "if Brad says that's all they want, you'd better trust him."

"But where is he? Why did he leave?" Her voice became a whine. "He should've stayed —"

"He was going to talk to Running Elk."

"At the reservation? But he'll be killed!" she wailed. "Why didn't you talk him out of it? You always seem to have a hold on him —"

"Linda, that's the whole point. Running Elk knows what's going on, and Brad wants to find out so he can tell us!" *I know I sound like a carping old maid but what else can I say to her?* she thought. She never dreamed this

71

was the kind of woman Brad wanted.

She turned abruptly and joined Sally and Emmy Lou who had gotten up from their knees, their faces shining with the assuredness of faith.

Just then Uncle Jimmie Watson barreled in, his strong voice booming across the room.

"The Cheyenne have left for the reservation. We don't know what's happening there, but we hope all's well with our Kaw friends."

Linda drew her breath sharply. "But that's where Brad Bennett —"

"Don't get all upset, miss!" he cut in sharply. "The least you can do is be thankful you're safe. Now quit your snivelin' and pray he'll get back to us."

Mrs. Metzker called from the door that the Cheyenne had all left, and one of the men had stopped by to report that some of the town's folk were watching the fight from the hill.

Annamarie's heart skipped a beat with the news as she tried to stifle the small knot of fear that nagged at her. Had Brad run into a hornet's nest by going to see Running Elk? *At this point all I can do is to trust the Lord to care for His own,* she told herself.

The women in the room seemed more

controlled and she breathed a prayer of thanks.

Half an hour later, Jacob Barth walked in, his rugged face damp with sweat. "The fight is over, as far as we can tell. It's lucky Captain Mullins and his troops arrived in time to help the Kaws. We think the Cheyennes are scared off and have gone."

"If only Brad is safe," Linda wailed in a small voice. "It looks to me the Kaws brought all this on themselves. They should've known better than to involve us!"

"If the Kaws hadn't been our friends," Emmy Lou hissed in Linda's ear, "who knows what the Cheyennes would have done to us — to you!"

Just then Brad swung through the door, his eager boyishness outlining every angle of his face.

"Well, relax, folks. The skirmish is over. Running Elk says one Cheyenne was killed and one Kaw wounded. Captain Mullins and his men showed those Cheyennes who was boss. They slunk away and headed west of town. I hope they won't raid the ranches!"

Suddenly he marched straight up to Annamarie and took her arm. "Annie," he began.

Linda rushed toward him and clung to his hand as she cried, "Brad, Brad, you were so brave, going to where the fighting was! Why didn't you think of . . . of me . . . of us! At least the awful Cheyennes won't bother us any more."

"No, Linda," Brad's face was grim. "The Indian menace in Kansas isn't over. Maybe here we're safe now, but in the Saline Valley the newly settled farmers aren't so lucky. The Cheyennes are raiding and murdering as they go. Captain Mullins said they've killed little children before their mothers' eyes and tomahawked fathers, then carried off the women. It's just too awful!" He shuddered and turned once more to Annamarie. "Sometimes I feel I should join General Sheridan and help end all the Indian trouble in Kansas to protect women like you from the hostile warriors." He paused and a grim look etched his face. "They're gone from here but as I started to tell you, Annie, they've kidnapped Po-a-be! I'm so sorry."

"Oh, God, no!" She whispered hoarsely. Po-a-be — her friend — gone! Annamarie's eyes blurred with tears and she turned away. *Oh, dear God — not Po-a-be!*

CHAPTER 7

Day after weary day Annamarie moped around the house, grieving over the disappearance of her Indian friend. The slim, brown figure that had endeared herself to Annamarie had been snatched away unceremoniously when the Cheyennes left.

What could I have done to avert it? Annamarie agonized mentally. Maybe I should've insisted she stay with us. But Po-a-be was an independent, loyal person to her Indian family as well as a vital part of Annamarie's life.

She recalled when they had first met. It was even before she had gone away to school. After the Indian mission was no longer used for a school and before the Brown Jug, Po-a-be had come. She was quiet and shy and found it hard to mingle with the white pupils until Annamarie had invited her to join in a girls' game of Drop-the-Handkerchief. As a result the girl had often visited the Tates when she came from the reservation, and soon became a natural part of the Council Grove community.

When Annamarie had left for Illinois to stay with her grandparents, Po-a-be had felt lost, Emmy Lou said later. The first person to meet the stagecoach when Annamarie returned was her little brown Indian friend. They trusted each other and often shared secrets. Annamarie sighed. Would she ever see her friend again?

"I must pray for her safety, and that she will escape," she told her mother who was stirring up a batch of cornbread as Annamarie cleaned the top of the stove.

"I know you miss her, but there's nothing that can be done to bring her back without God's intervention," Sara Tate said, whacking the dough with firm strokes before pouring it into a pan.

"Perhaps she'll try to escape from the Cheyennes," Annamarie said hopefully as she wiped the grime from the black range with a rag. "And when she does, I'll tell her of God's love. Somehow I don't think I ever let her know that God loves the Indians as much as He does the white men. We seem to think we have a monopoly on God. Yet she was so sensitive to my feelings . . ."

Annamarie smiled, remembering the time Po-a-be had come to warn them about the Cheyennes' impending raid and had mentioned Brad "liked her." Po-a-be had told her to warn Brad because she was concerned. And Brad?

She sighed again. It seemed ever since the Cheyenne attack, Linda had become more possessive of Brad. It was as though she thought she had every right to him. Well, maybe she did. Again the sight of Linda in Brad's arms on the cliff flashed before her eyes and his strong words that she'd always have him.

In church Linda made sure she sat with him, spreading her full ruffled skirts over her knees, almost touching Brad's legs. If Linda meant nothing to him, he should have had the courage to tell Annamarie. During the Indian raid when Brad had found her at Hebrank's Brewery, his comment to Annamarie, "If anything had happened to you," was left unfinished in her mind. Annamarie wondered how he would have finished the sentence if she hadn't brought up Linda's name. But he had quickly commented on his concern for her, too. He seemed to want both of them. *And I'm too . . . stubborn, is it? . . . to share him with her! He'll have to make up his mind one of these days whom he wants,* she decided.

It was Sunday morning again and as Annamarie and Susan walked up the path to the Brown Jug, Linda stood in the doorway clutching Brad's arm possessively. Annamarie caught the flash in her green eyes that plainly warned, *He's mine, and you know it!* Holding her blond head high, she marched Brad inside. He looked into Linda's piquant face and leaned over and whispered something into her ear.

Annamarie's heart sank. Whatever hopes she'd had of a future with him were dashed. He showed no sign of denying it. The church service that Sunday was meaningless to her and she heard almost nothing of it except the praise to God for having spared the town during the raid.

After church Brad slipped up behind Annamarie and grabbed her shoulders. "Annie, you'll sing with me next Sunday, won't you? It's been awhile since we've sung together."

She turned, startled. "I . . . I'm sorry." She moved away.

"Wait!" he called. "I'd like to talk —"

"I have nothing to say to you, Bradford Bennett," she said coldly, and walked away.

Why did I say that? Oh, dear God, I hurt so much! She felt her heart shatter into a million stabbing pieces. Grabbing Susan's hand, she started down the street, walking briskly.

"What's the matter, Annamarie?" asked Susan.

"Oh, it's nothing worth mentioning," Annamarie answered.

"Does it have to do with Brad Bennett?" she prodded.

"I should've known," Annamarie began, "if he likes frail, helpless creatures, then he deserves her, and I'm not for him. I guess this means I must be strong and somehow survive the pain in my heart."

"Who's frail and helpless? What pain in your heart?" asked Susan.

"I guess you're too young to understand about these things right now," she sniffed back.

She was quiet at the dinner table as she and her mother served the chicken corn stew that swam with cubed potatoes.

Will Johnson ate heartily, then wiped his mouth with the fine linen napkin and pushed himself away from the table. "That was a fine meal, Miz Tate," he said, getting to his feet. "If you'll excuse me, I must go down to the *Advertiser* office and work on my next editorial. I have not quite decided if I should write about the tragedy of the Indian girl's capture or the bravery at Hebrank Brewery. Both were outstanding feats." He picked up his hat from behind the door and left.

Annamarie got out the dishpan and began to clear the table, with her mind on both subjects. She knew the people who had shown such strength during the grim morning of the raid should be commended; yet the loss of her faithful Indian friend was felt very deeply. As she poured hot water into the dishpan, she paused to wipe her eyes with the corner of her pink-checked apron.

"You're so quiet, Annamarie," her mother said, picking up the tea towel. "You've seemed very troubled ever since we came home from church. Is anything wrong?"

"Oh, Mother," she choked out. "I . . . I don't know what to think! Brad and I — we once were a pair of faithful friends before he went away to college. Now that he's home, we're almost . . . strangers."

"I see. And Linda Corling seems to have taken over. Well, dear, if you're God's choice for Brad, He will bring it to pass no matter how many Lindas come into his life. But if you're not, you're better off that you know it now."

Annamarie wiped the table and hung up the dishpan on its nail. She knew her mother was right. But why did it have to be so hard?

"Thank you, Mother. You're right, of course."

Without a word, she went upstairs to the small bedroom she shared with Susan. One thing she knew she had to do. She must write a letter to Brad and tell him what was on her heart. If he knew how she felt about this confusing situation, he'd have to clear it up, one way or another. She'd put the letter in their "post office" niche in the Hermit's Cave. He'd find it and explain everything if there was anything to explain.

She recalled that April afternoon before she'd left for Illinois when the group of young people had ridden home late from Clear Ridge on their ponies after a last day of school celebration. The boys and girls broke up in pairs and rode together slowly. The tender pink and green of the landscape with the sunset tinting the sky overhead, and all the far south and west stretching away into waves of misty green melting to amethyst wove a magic over the world all its own.

She and Brad had reached the draw beyond the big cottonwood, and had led their ponies by the bridle reins where they lingered and gathered fragrant bouquets of prairie lilies and mauve windflowers, and played like two children among the spicy blooms.

Brad had formed a crude crown of blossoms and laid it on her dark curls. The purple twilight, shot through with sunset coloring, had made a glory overhead she'd never forget. The air was very sweet, and the draw was still and dewy in the midst of the wide prairie.

That's when Brad had looked into her deep blue eyes and said softly, "Oh, Annie . . ." and had kissed her red lips softly just once. It had seemed like a declaration of love. She had never forgotten it.

They had both left Council Grove shortly after that, he to Ohio for college and she for her grandparents' for her education. That was also when he'd asked her to wait for him. Somehow she had cupped the memory of that exquisite moment in her heart. They had both been very young then — perhaps too young.

But now. . . . She sighed, and a pain stabbed her heart again. He seemed torn between his duty to their long-ago friendship and his attraction to the tall, silky-haired Linda.

She drew a sheet of paper from her desk and began to write. Words couldn't express her feelings and she tore up one draft after another. Finally what she wanted to say came clearly.

Brad —
Perhaps too much time had passed since we first met, or maybe I put too much stock into our once-youthful

emotions. Apparently you have grown away from me and no longer feel about me as you once did. But I simply cannot go on clinging to the declaration of your youthful love, because it's obvious that you no longer feel toward me the same as you once did, and Linda Corling has no doubt captured your heart. I'm asking you to end our once tender friendship so you can concentrate on your relationship with her. Please don't try to see me again, unless —

She wiped her eyes as she recopied the words, folded the paper into neat quarters and tucked it into her apron pocket. Then with a determined thrust to her chin she left the house and headed up the cliff path. The bluff with its rock-strewn path was often full of surprises, both delightful and scary. Centipedes and rattlesnakes in particular made their homes in its crevices. The footing was precarious to the climber if one wasn't careful. In the past Brad had held her hand as they had scrambled up that path together.

When she reached the top and made her way carefully to the cave, she gulped back a sob. This was the end of her friendship with Brad Bennett unless he responded to her note.

If he really cared, he'd write to tell her so.

As the weeks passed and she received no word from Brad, she grew more disheartened than ever. No doubt he had decided to ignore it. That should be answer enough, she figured.

The work at the boarding house kept her busy. Another boarder had taken the extra bed in Will Johnson's room and now there were two extra places to set at the table, two more sets of clothes to launder. F.B. Nichols had been hired to teach in the new graded school and had asked about a place to board. Sara Tate offered to board him. Still, the extra money barely covered expenses. Annamarie had prayed for some way to earn the needed money.

One hot July afternoon after Annamarie had scrubbed the kitchen floor and hung up fresh tea towels, she was startled by a brisk knock at the front door. As she opened it, two strange men stood on the porch twisting their hats in their hands.

They introduced themselves as Buck Willis and John Fromm.

"We've come from Clear Ridge school," the dark-bearded Willis began rather seriously. "We hear you have a college eddication."

"Yup, and as we're lookin' for a schoolmarm for our school, we wondered if maybe you —"

"They's about twenty children and we'd be most obliged —"

"We provide room and board, plus a reasonable pay," the tall, lanky Fromm finished with a grin.

Taken aback by this surprising turn of events, Annamarie invited them into the house. She was glad she had dusted the parlor that morning and had washed the scrim curtains only two days ago.

"Why. . . . I —" she motioned them to the settee. "I certainly would consider such a position. I had no idea you were looking for a teacher."

"Our last year's schoolmarm up and got married and moved away. We was stumped, 'til we heard you might be available," Willis said.

She was overwhelmed with the idea. She had never planned to teach school, but some of her college curriculum would prove helpful, and here was the perfect solution to help her mother. Clear Ridge was some ten miles north with the boarding place provided for.

"I'm interested in your offer," she said again, after she caught her breath. "Perhaps I can ride back and forth weekends. Since my father's death, my mother has been struggling to make a living for my sister and me."

"Then it's settled!" John Fromm said, unfolding his lanky figure like a jackknife as he stood up. "We'd like you to come in mid-August a few days early. You're to attend one day at Kansas State Normal at Emporia. We like our teachers to know all they can. School starts the last day of August, if the pupils don't have to help on the farm."

"Ben and Lizzie Powers will be boardin' you," Willis said. "They live just beyond the school. We'll see you in a week then!"

After they left the house, Annamarie was almost giddy with excitement.

"Mother! Mother!" she shouted as she went in search of Mrs. Tate who was sorting potatoes in the lean-to. "Guess what? I have a teaching job, and I'll be able to help out with our income!"

Sara Tate fumbled with a potato in her hand. "But Annamarie, I didn't expect you to help earn our living. With two boarders now, if we pinch carefully —"

"That's just it, Mother. This way you won't have to struggle quite so hard. And I'll make some use of the education I received in Illinois that you and Father helped provide. You'll manage the work with Susan's help, I'm sure. And it's a real answer to our prayers."

When she told Emmy Lou, her friend was aghast. "Annamarie, are you out of your mind? You mean, you'll go away from Council Grove? Your mother and sister —"

She laughed. "Not for good. Just during the week. And it's because we need the money!"

"Well, if you ask me, you're just *inviting* that snooty Linda Corling to grab Brad Bennett for herself if you're not here to stop her!"

"That . . . that's entirely up to Brad," she said with a faltering sigh, "If he cares about her more than me, well, what can I do about it?"

A shiver went through Annamarie at the thought. Thus far he hadn't responded to her note, and she couldn't understand it. The next move was Brad's.

CHAPTER 8

The *Advertiser*'s headlines carried news of the forthcoming Topeka rally. It was to be a big political meeting in the State Capitol. The Indian menace in the Saline Valley had grown into a pernicious evil as unprotected settlements scattered throughout Northwest Kansas were threatened and raided. The Kansas citizens were outraged and the rally would bring them together to make some important decisions.

As additional news of the atrocities drifted in almost daily, Annamarie felt an undercurrent of uneasiness and restlessness sweep over the town. Just what it was, she couldn't tell, but Brad and Jeremy and Ed Keitch and some of the other boys were often huddled under the elm, their faces solemn. She knew Brad had strong convictions about the issue — something she couldn't quite understand. She overheard some of their conversations as things got worse.

It was true. The Cheyennes under Black Kettle were sweeping across the state, hoping to take back the land they felt the white man had stolen from them. When she thought of how they had kidnapped Po-a-be, Annamarie could almost agree they should be subdued. But why must all this affect Council Grove so far away? And where *was* Po-a-be? Would she ever see her Indian friend again?

Her days were busy, going over her meager wardrobe as she tried to repair her clothes that would befit a school teacher. The gay blue and green plaid was most appropriate, for it would show the dirt less quickly, although the simple pinked-checked gingham with its rounded collar was quite serviceable.

With a sinking heart she realized Brad had still not answered her note. What did it mean?

"I can't understand it," she confessed to Emmy Lou who had come to help her with the sewing. The two girls sat in the shady side of Tates' house under the spreading oak. "I hardly see him. He seems to be occupied with his work at the bank. He seldom shows up in town outside of work — except to speak soberly with the other boys."

"Oh, I can believe he's busy at the bank," her friend snorted delicately as she bit off her thread with strong white teeth. "What about Linda Corling?"

"What of her?"

"She's not been hanging onto his arm lately?"

Annamarie let out a deep sigh. "I don't know. We have not had a youth outing in some weeks. When I walk down to the store and I meet her, she pitty-pats down the aisles in her dainty finery and big, wide-brimmed hats like she owns the place. She scarcely has a word for me."

"I think you're foolish to go away from Council Grove and leave her to Brad. If you stayed around —"

"But it's a chance I have to take to help out with Mother's money problems, Emmy Lou," Annamarie said, smoothing out the hem she'd finished in the apple-green challis. "Besides, the Lord may have other plans for me. Perhaps I'm to teach school instead of thinking of marriage." She sighed again.

"And be an old maid schoolmarm?" Emmy Lou snapped off her thread with a vengeance. "That goes for me since no one ever asks to take me out. But I'll never believe God wants you to make teaching your life! I'd always felt you were right for Brad, and he was right for you and that some day . . ." Her voice trailed off.

"There's no doubt in my mind that if this is to happen, the next move is Brad's. So far, he hasn't tried to contact me."

"You told him you didn't want to see him anymore, didn't you? So what *can* he think?"

Annamarie bit her lower lip sharply. "But if he really cared, he'd at least try."

Oh, it seemed so futile. For now, she had to put Brad out of her mind and concentrate on her job as a teacher. On Sunday afternoon she was to ride out to Clear Ridge to become acquainted with her new work. This seemed God's answer to her prayers to help her mother.

She dressed carefully Sunday morning, brushed back her long, thick brown hair and coiled it low on her neck. The hot August sun beat fiercely as she walked to church between Susan and her mother, and she pulled down the brim of her black straw hat.

The Brown Jug bustled with worshippers dressed in their summery ginghams and freshly ironed delaines. As Annamarie, her mother and sister went into the church she led them to a row of seats near the front. She looked around quickly. There was no sign of Brad, Jeremy or Ed. They were always prompt and faithful. Then she saw Linda, looking paler than ever in her white eyelet dress with its billowing skirt and low-cut neckline.

After the singing, Pastor Nash bowed his head for prayer. Then he opened his Bible.

"Before we go into the message, let's pray for our young men who have gone to the Topeka rally," he began. "With the Indians becoming more and more hostile, our young men have become increasingly concerned. They need the Lord's guidance in the decisions they face."

Annamarie's mind spun. Were the boys really planning to fight Black Kettle and his murderous horde?

Linda Corling swept up beside her when church was over. "Did you know Brad and the others planned to go to the rally?" she whispered in Annamarie's ear.

"I knew he was thinking of it," she said quietly. "Did you know?"

"Well . . . of course, he doesn't tell me everything!" Linda flung out. "But why would he be so . . . so crazy to leave his good position at the bank to go on a wild goose chase?"

Annamarie took a deep breath. "Brad has always had strong convictions, Linda. I know he prays about what God wants him to do. The decision to fight is his own — not mine, not yours!"

She whirled around and walked away. As if she could influence Brad one way or another! This afternoon she was to leave Council Grove to ride out to Clear Ridge to prepare to teach, and whatever Brad and his friends planned to do was their business. At least he hadn't confided in Linda what these plans were.

After the noon meal of fried prairie chicken and generous helpings of cooked carrots, Annamarie tied her few belongings into a flour sack, packed a saddle bag with school supplies and hung them on Lady's side. The two hungry boarders had eaten heartily and had already left for the day.

The ten-mile ride to the Clear Ridge community would be hot, and she jammed a sturdy blue sunbonnet on her head.

"I'll be back on Friday," she told her mother, "after I've settled in. Just leave anything you can't manage until I come back."

She swung herself onto Lady's back and rode out of town.

The hot August dust hung like a pall over the land. High, cauliflower clouds seemed to hang overhead without movement. The landscape grew more drab and faded as she rode down the dusty prairie. A dull feeling settled over her and she wiped a lone tear that trickled down her cheeks. Somehow she felt more depressed than ever.

What had she let herself in for, to leave her home and her beloved family and friends, for a lonely, forsaken community where she didn't know a soul?

She wiped her eyes with the back of her long gray sleeve and took a deep breath. "Lord, You led me to take this job, and I must depend upon You to strengthen me for it," she prayed. "You've said, 'I'll never leave nor forsake you,' so I'm taking You at Your word."

Swallowing her dismay, she rode up the last hill with determination toward the white-painted schoolhouse. Her boarding place lay just beyond, according to John Fromm. She hoped Ben and Lizzie Powers were aware that she was coming.

The scrappy little farm that lay ahead looked as forlorn as a tired old woman. When she rode into the yard, a mangy shepherd dog trotted out to meet her.

Ben Powers, tall and gaunt with balding, grizzled gray hair, came out of the house.

"You the new schoolmarm?" he asked as she pulled Lady's reins to a stop. "We knew you was comin' today. If it weren't so tarnally hot and dry. Hey, Maw, Teacher's come!" he hollered.

The woman's slightly stooped figure stepped onto the porch and hurried toward Annamarie, both arms outstretched.

"Welcome, Miz Tate. It's right good to have you come. You're a sight for sore eyes.

Here, Ben, help her with her stuff and put her horse up. You must be right tuckered out," she added.

Annamarie slid lightly to the ground and took Lizzie's puckered little hand. "It's good to see you, too, Mrs. Powers. Yes, it was a long, tiring ride, and I'd be grateful for a fresh drink of water."

Lizzie scurried inside for a cup and worked the pump handle up and down. Annamarie took the fresh drink from Lizzie's hand and drank it almost in one gulp. Then she wiped her mouth with her sleeve.

"Here, come inside and set down and rest, Miz Tate. You must be plumb wore out."

Lizzie led her into the tiny house and drew out a kitchen chair. The room was scrupulously clean, with red-checkered curtains dallying at the open windows. There was a pinched look about the room. Yet an air of hominess permeated the simple furnishings and the clean-scrubbed floors.

"Please call me Annamarie," she said, setting down her cup. "I'm not used to being so formal."

From the beginning the couple insisted she call them by their first names. "You just call me Ben," the old man said tartly. "That's what ever'body in these parts does."

Although he seemed rather distant at first,

Annamarie soon learned that no one in Clear Ridge was more loyal to Kansas, to the Union and to God than Ben Powers.

"And don't forget — my name's Lizzie."

The tiny woman with dark sparkly eyes constituted many virtues rolled into one: good, kind, patient, gentle and long-suffering. And she soon discovered that Lizzie was usually busy with her daily round of chores including the chickens, canning, cooking and cleaning. And clucking after Ben.

"You hafta get acquainted with your pupils," Lizzie told her as she set the tea kettle on to boil. "Take the Fields now. Roxy has adenoids. It affects the way she pernounces her words. And Herman Kohfeld's a stubborn one. And the Chases. Poor as church mice. And there's them Culp twins — Typhena and Tryphosa — Bible names, you know. But they's called Phenie and Phosie. Alike as two peas in a pod. You need to get to know them. Oh — and the Kremeiers —"

"First I'll get settled," Annamarie said. "Then I must begin to plan my lessons and visit the schoolhouse, too."

"Yes, and there's to be a cakewalk next week," Lizzie said. "The whole community's comin' to it to raise money for school needs. You'll meet lots of those folks there. Now just tuck your things away while I fix supper.

Take off those hot boots and put on some-thin' more comf'table. There's your bed-room through that door."

The bedroom was tiny but clean with a neatly-made iron bedstead. She drew off her long-sleeved dress and slipped into a cool, short-sleeved summer shift. She hung up her other clothes on the nails in the corner and placed her clean underwear in the drawers of the bureau.

She smiled a little as she pondered the upcoming events. She was to attend a com-munity cakewalk and the Teacher's Institute in the next two weeks. She knew from her visits in Illinois that a cakewalk was like a folk game in which couples promenaded to musical accompaniment — until the music stopped. Whoever stopped at a designated signal received a generous slice of cake. And the Institute was to acquaint her with the latest learning methods. Maybe it would be a good year after all.

She dug out her meager school supplies and began to prepare lesson plans until Liz-zie rapped sharply on the bedroom door.

"Supper's ready. Come and eat!"

The meal was plain: potato soup, freshly baked bread and stewed apples. Annamarie realized how hungry she was as she sat down at the table.

"Have s'more," insisted Ben after Annamarie complimented Lizzie on the soup. After dinner she was so tired that as soon as she could excuse herself, she went to bed.

The air that blew through the open window was stifling hot. As she lay there staring at the dark ceiling, she thought about the past few hours, and a slight shiver swept over her in spite of the heat. She had never felt so alone, so far away from family and friends, and underneath it all was the gnawing pain of Brad's obvious unconcern for her. That he had left for the rally without telling her added to her dismay — yet somehow she knew God had led her here.

Dear Lord, she prayed in the darkness, *I don't know what I'm doing here, but I know You wanted me to come. Please be with Brad . . . and please direct my life,* she prayed again.

CHAPTER 9

Annamarie came home late Friday evening, tired but full of enthusiasm. Wednesday at the Teachers' Institute had gone well and sharpened her interest in the job she was facing. School would begin officially next week.

The prairie lay quiet and gray in the early evening, with tufts of dusty goldenrod and daisies drooping on limp stems in the late August heat. Cattle grazed along the banks of the Neosho, shaking their heads at the biting insects.

Lady trotted dutifully along the trail that led into town and turned up Pine Street as though she knew where to go by instinct.

Annamarie had barely stabled the mare when she heard a familiar chuckle, and looked up to see Brad's merry face framed in the upper half of the Dutch door.

"Hullo, Annie!" he said with his usual warmth. "We just got back from the rally in Topeka and I had this urge to tell you about it. How's Clear Ridge's favorite teacher?"

Annamarie finished pouring a gallon of oats into Lady's feed trough. "School doesn't start until next week," she said, picking up her small bag. "I'm getting settled there. I spent one day in Emporia at Kansas State Normal School for a Teacher's Institute. Even though I graduated from the academy a year ago, I still have much to learn."

"Oh, you'll do fine. You can cope with anything."

"I hope so," she shrugged and smiled.

"Jeremy, Ed and I have been absolutely appalled by the Indian atrocities in the Saline and Solomon Valleys. When I heard this man, Morton, at the rally talk about all the horror, it made my blood run cold. The Cheyennes are murdering everyone in their path. Unprotected settlers are butchered right and left. Most of the settlers are discharged Union soldiers who're homesteading on the Plains. The government in Washington is either ignorant or indifferent to this outrage. It was awful, Morton said."

"But that's so far removed from Council Grove. How can that affect us here?"

His gaze strayed to the west. The setting sun was sinking through a colorless sky and the rippling waves of the prairies seemed shorn of their usual glory. Annamarie shifted her position to hear Brad's reply when he finally spoke.

"According to Morton, Cheyenne braves under Black Kettle rode from the southwest, threatening every unguarded village. Then they straggled, dirty and ragged, into Fort Hays claiming to be 'good Indians.' The army felt sorry for them and took them in. After feasting on beans and coffee, they skedaddled. The next morning they were raiding more settlements and killing more settlers. This outrage must stop!"

"Can't the government do anything? It would seem —"

"Oh, Governor Crawford and the governor of Colorado have urged Washington to take action but they've done nothing. So General Sheridan has decided to act, together with Colonel Forsythe. The Kansas 19th Cavalry at Fort Harker is ready to organize troops and move against the enemy."

She leaned against the barn door and drew a deep breath. "And just how does this affect you, Brad Bennett? Why are you telling me this?"

He folded his brawny arms across his chest and his brown eyes took on a faraway look.

"Do you plan to join the Kansas 19th, Brad?" She tried to swallow the lump in her throat.

"Annie," he drew a long breath, "it's so hard to decide. All I know is, this fierce raiding and rampaging must stop! But because I love you so very deeply, I know that if I join this fight I might never come back, for it will be a fight to the finish. Annie, what shall I do?"

The passionate glow in his brown eyes startled her. Did she hear what she thought she heard? He had never actually declared his love for her until now.

"I'm sure you've prayed about this, Brad. Surely the Lord will show you."

"Oh, yes. I've argued with myself, and agonized earnestly about this and so have Jeremy and Ed. For my part I'd be glad to go and put this to an end. I think you'd agree I should. Am I right?"

She nodded almost imperceptibly. "If you really feel you should go, then go, by all means. But why are you asking me?"

He shook his dark curls. "It's good to know you're with me in this. But what keeps me from making up my mind is knowing how this will upset Linda. You're her friend. If you could —"

Annamarie stiffened. Linda? Her friend? She doubted that. So, he was still thinking more of Linda than of her. Without a word, she swung around abruptly and ran toward the house.

So he was using her to win Linda's approval! "Well, I can't do it, Lord. I just can't do it!" she cried. She hurried toward the light shining through the kitchen window to her family waiting inside.

"Annamarie, where were you?" her mother turned away from the stove when she came in. "We heard you ride up, and when you didn't come in, I began to worry."

Annamarie paused to hug her mother briefly. A sandy-haired young man got up from the table and came toward her.

"Your mother's been worried. I'm Graham Scott, one of the new boarders. If there's anything I can do to help —"

She drew back quickly. "Thank you, Mr. Scott. But I . . . I just received some bad news. While I was feeding the horse, Brad Bennett came by. He told me he and two other Grove boys are seriously thinking of joining the Kansas Cavalry. This means vicious fighting!"

She sank wearily into a chair by the table.

"Jesus hated injustice in His day, and I'm sure God won't let this Indian menace continue if we strike back," Scott said as he sat down again.

Where have I heard his name before? Annamarie puzzled. *This must be the new assistant Indian agent who was coming. Didn't he also pastor a small congregation on the other side of town?* she wondered.

She was quiet as her mother filled her bowl with creamed noodles, flavored with bits of sausage and beans. So, this made three boarders for her mother. She was glad for her sake although this would cramp the house more than ever.

"So are you getting settled at Clear Ridge?" her mother inquired.

Susan followed with a dozen more questions. Annamarie gave them a report on her week although her mind kept straying to thoughts of her conversation with Brad at the stable. Before long it was bedtime.

During the Sunday morning church service, Annamarie avoided Brad. The pain in her heart was too deep from Friday evening when he had declared his devotion for her in one breath, but showed his feelings for Linda in the next.

She caught his gaze upon her face several times during the sermon but turned away. *Lord, why does he expect me to stand by Linda who seems to have captured his heart when I love him so much? Oh, it's so hard to see him leave to join the Calvary, but it must reveal his deep commitment to You by trying to do the right thing.*

After lunch she told her mother she wanted to be alone, and when she had cleared the dishes she took her bonnet from its nail behind the kitchen door and hurried out into the pressing August heat. She thought perhaps he had left a letter for her in their "post office," and she sped up the cliff path, wondering if he had answered her note.

The midday heat soon tired her and she slowed her stride to a walk. She remembered Graham Scott's words to her just this morning. There had been cheer and strength in his rich, resonant voice when he said to her, "Little girl, please don't worry about anything. All the tangles will straighten for you. Be patient. There's sunshine behind those clouds."

She found her way to the cave. A thick tangle of vines nearly concealed it. It was merely a deep recess under an overhanging shelf of rock, but penetrated far enough into the cliff to walk inside. Stooping into the cool, dim opening, she stepped over to the crevice and groped for an envelope. She fumbled more deeply until she felt a square sheet of paper. With trembling fingers she drew it out and unfolded it. It was the letter she had written to Brad weeks ago! No wonder he hadn't answered it! Perhaps his large hands had not been able to reach in far enough to retrieve it.

Slowly she crushed the letter then walked out into the sunlight and threw the letter into the bushes. Then she made her way carefully down the steep path back to the house.

After packing her clean clothes into the shabby valise, she went downstairs and talked with her mother and Susan for awhile before leaving. Then she told them goodbye and saddled Lady for the return trip to Clear Ridge. A steady wind had picked up and the ride back to the Powers farm seemed to go faster.

Ben and Lizzie were happy to see her return. They welcomed her with a tasty meal of fried prairie chickens and dumplings, and she picked up life where she had left off the previous week. Her first day of teaching had almost arrived and she felt a few butterflies in her stomach. Would she be able to do it? She recalled Brad's words, "You can cope with anything."

The next morning she walked to the schoolhouse. A tangle of underbrush clung to the windows and the red leaves from the scrub oak and wild sumac appeared to set fire to the walls. Once inside, she laid her books on the desk. The desks were hand-hewn and scarred, and a water pail with a long-handled dipper stood on a built-in shelf in one corner.

She had just taken out her sheaf of lesson plans when she heard a scuffling up the gravel path.

Roxy Field arrived first, her blond hair all neatly-braided. She swept up to Annamarie's desk, blowing in with an air of, "Well, here I am!"

"Good bordig, Teacher!" Roxy sang out, thumping her books onto one of the knife-scarred desks. Her scrawny brother Jack trotted after her like a faithful puppy.

"Good bordig"? Oh, the adenoids, Annamarie thought.

"Good morning, Roxy."

"Are you Biss Tate?"

"Yes, I'm Miss Tate."

Johnny Case slammed into the room just then, clean and patched and darned, followed by Jed Kremeier's flock of four, smelling of boiled cabbage. She could stand the long, narrow classroom that smelled of musty chalk and fresh paint on the wainscoting, but the boiled cabbage smell almost overwhelmed her.

One by one the other pupils arrived, and her fears were beginning to subside. She found herself facing a battery of twenty pairs of eyes, but discovered later that only nineteen eyes stared back at her. Jakie Willis had become too curious with a firecracker one summer and, as a result, wore a glass eye. He gladly removed it for the entertainment of anyone who paid him a cent.

The Culp twins were identical as Lizzie had said, but Phenie had a mole above her right eye so Annamarie could tell them apart. All in all, it was an extremely hot, squirmy, perspiring bunch. Roxy Field told her right away that she taught "differdly from last year's teacher." Herman Kohfeld got a stubborn streak and sat with his lower lip hanging down like the endgate from the back of a spring wagon. What does one do with a boy like that? She decided to ignore him and it had good results — he hauled up the endgate and became the most agreeable student for the rest of the day.

When the day was almost over, Roxy told her they always sang the "beddidiction," which Annamarie interpreted to mean "benediction." Students stood by their desks and bowed their heads.

> *"Now the day is over,*
> *night is drawing nigh.*
> *Guide us in Thy mercy*
> *Hear the children's cry . . ."*

It touched her that their final gathering of the day was before God's throne, casting their little burdens upon Him. At first it had been only a job for her, but now she quietly cast herself before the Father's throne and prayed silently, "Lord, I'll do my best if You'll help me."

The minute she dismissed them, the twenty pairs of feet scraped and clattered toward the door.

"See you at the cakewalk tonight!" She heard the words from all twenty pupils as they bounded away.

The cakewalk! Annamarie remembered the Powers' mention of this community effort to raise money for school supplies. According to her Institute professor's admonition, it was important to suit each individual's needs. More money for supplies would help her accomplish that goal. Knowing she was expected to be at this evening's event put a slight damper upon her enthusiasm.

She dressed carefully after supper, wearing her second-best blue delaine with its lace-edged collar and full puffed sleeves. She brushed her thick hair until it shone and coiled it at the nape of her neck.

Glancing into the tiny mirror above the bureau, she noticed the tiredness in her eyes. Yes, she was weary. But there was also a tinge of sadness.

Lizzie had decided to stay home with a

bad case of "rhematiz," so Ben and Anna-marie walked together in the early dusk toward the schoolhouse. Long flushed clouds of sunset had darkened and the coolness of the evening lay still in the air.

Already the schoolhouse swarmed with people dressed in clean, crisply ironed clothes — all except tiny Mae Kremeier, who wore the same wrinkled dress she'd worn all day. They all milled around, murmuring and muttering with neighborly bits of gossip. The screech of fiddles and the twang of guitars and a harmonica or two meant they were tuning up, and the notes rose above the hubbub of voices. Lantern light glimmered from the walls sifting a dim light over the room. She stood hesitantly near the door and noticed the desks had been shoved into one corner.

"Ever'body find your partners for the first walk!" John Fromm's loud voice cut through the din. "Folks, remember to meet the new teacher while you're at it. She's a purty little thing, so don't be bashful and leave her standin' on the sidelines!"

The music began, and in a flash a chubby young man with a cheerful face and a shock of straw-colored hair was at her side.

"You wanna have the first walk with me? The name's Harry Jensen." He grabbed her arm before she could protest, plunked down his dime, then started to squire her briskly around the room. The laughter, the scrape of feet, the giggles and gay banter rose all around her. She felt Harry's hand tighten on her elbow as he guided her expertly around the room to the lilting, twanging fiddle and guitar as they scraped out an agonizing version of "Turkey in the Straw." Suddenly the music stopped. A wooden rod had mysteriously appeared in front of them.

"Oh, it's Teacher and Harry what's won the first piece of cake!" someone yelled, and applause ripped across the room. Annamarie felt her face flame. She was sure this was preplanned. Of course, "Teacher" was destined to win the first favored slice of cake.

Harry carried her plate and steered her to one corner. "Now Miss Tate, you'n' me, we'll get acquainted. It means you'd better not refuse other walks with me t'night. I found you first!"

Laughter spilled everywhere. She seemed a captive of this straw-haired boy who felt he'd made a conquest. Not only a piece of cake, but a "girl" as well!

The room grew stifling, and she moved closer to the open window for a breath of fresh air. To be polite, she knew she was expected to participate in this folk frolic and be available to "walk" with anyone who asked her.

The next several "walks" seemed like trophies won by other young men of the community, but Harry kept his promise and returned for "the next one" often.

Laughing, chatting couples flirting with their partners surged around constantly, and she was never without some young swain at her side as the fiddle squeaked and screeched, trying to be heard above the loud laughter and chatter in the crowded room.

Harry grew more bold as he placed his arm gently around her shoulders. "This is the big event of the school year," he whispered in her ear. "I hope before the year's over, you'n' me's gonna look for a preacher!"

She pulled away from him. "Please, Harry. I don't . . . I'm not . . . you're not —"

"You're right. I'm not a bad sort. Fact is, I'm considered quite a catch here. I already have a nice homestead that I'm provin' up. You couldn't go wrong."

She shut out the noise, the boisterous laughter, the crude music and looked around wildly. People on the sidelines were watching the couples whirl to a fast trot as the music speeded up.

Suddenly Annamarie froze. One face in the crowd on the sidelines seemed achingly familiar. It looked like Brad's. It *was* Brad's! She shoved Harry aside as she tried to push her way through the crowd. *I must talk to him,* she thought. In a flash he had vanished. No, it must've been someone else who only looked like Brad.

The rest of the evening passed in a blur and she was relieved when Ben appeared by her side.

"It's late, Annamarie, and we both got to go home and get some sleep," he said, and she nodded. John Fromm would lock up and blow out the lanterns, Ben told her as she followed him outside gratefully.

On the way out, Harry pressed close to her. "I'll be up one of these evenin's. You ain't seen the last of me yet," he grinned.

Her legs ached from constant motion, the countless "walks" around the room, and she grasped Ben's arm more tightly as they walked home silently in the dim moonlight.

When they came to the house, Lizzie was still up. She had put on her thin summer nightgown and braided her skimpy hair into wispy plaits and was seated in her rocker that moved lightly back and forth.

"You have a good time, Annamarie?" she said. "You had a couple of visitors. A fine-lookin' feller and a pair of other Grove boys was here lookin' for you. The handsome one said he wanted to tell you goodbye. That he was leavin' for the Saline Valley in the mornin' to fight the Cheyennes. I told him you was at the cakewalk. Did he find you?"

A sharp pain stabbed Annamarie and she gasped. So it really had been Brad — to tell her he had decided to go after all. She knew the fighting would be long and hard. What if she never saw him again?

CHAPTER 10

As tired as she was, Annamarie couldn't rest after she went to bed that night. She couldn't stop thinking about Brad and that he had come all the way to Clear Ridge to tell her goodbye. Obviously he had seen her in the company of Harry or one of the other boys at the cake-walk. He had no doubt decided she wanted nothing to do with him. But that wasn't true. She had to admit to herself that her jealousy of Linda had distorted her feelings for Brad. Now she was filled with regrets.

Oh, dear God, she prayed, *I know I was wrong not to trust him, but the fact that he seemed so concerned about Linda. . . . Why did I shut him out? Why didn't I try to be Linda's friend as he had asked me?* She stirred restlessly. *If only I could do it over.*

But Lizzie had said the boys were on their way to the Saline Valley, perhaps to join the calvary at Fort Harker. Fighting the relentless Cheyennes could have tragic results. She had to admit Brad had confessed to loving her last Friday, but it was so confusing to hear him continue to express his concern for Linda's feelings.

A warm breeze blew a few strands of hair across her face and she tossed and turned then stared out the window. The yellow prairie moon shone like an accusing eye through the curtains, and a sick, brassy feeling filled her mouth. How could she go on, knowing she had refused to trust Brad when he'd come to her, asking her to believe in him? She was so sure she was right in refusing to talk to him. Perhaps the Lord would have helped her, if she had been more tender, more gentle.

She recalled the verses in Proverbs: *Trust in the LORD with all thine heart; and lean not unto thine own understanding. In all thy ways acknowledge him, and he shall direct thy paths.* She agonized over the past events as scalding tears stung her eyes and trickled onto her pillow. She threw the sheet back and got up to get a handkerchief, then laid back down. All she could do was whisper, *Lord, help me. Please help me.*

In the laggard hours before dawn as the stars grew pale and reluctant, she finally dropped off to sleep.

In the morning she dressed carefully and set her chin firmly. She would try to put away her battered feelings and be the best teacher possible.

Lizzie looked at her sharply at breakfast. "I hope the news last night didn't rile you up too much. The good lookin' feller seemed awful set on seein' you."

"I . . . he apparently changed his mind after he got there because we didn't . . . meet."

"Well, if he'd really wanted to see you that bad, he'd 'a done it. Maybe he'd seen you was havin' a good time without him. Ben says you did, and that Harry Jensen seemed real took by you. He's a real nice boy, provin' his claim and homesteadin' and all. Maybe he can help you forget about them other fellers."

Annamarie didn't answer. She finished her breakfast, packed her lunch pail and started for the door. "I really won't have time to do much romancing with all the lesson preparation. I aim to be a good teacher, and to do that I must work hard," she said by the way of response.

Lizzie moved her tiny body toward the stove. "I'm sure you are a real hit with the children. From what Ben says —"

"I must be going, Lizzie," Annamarie cut in, and with a wave of her hand she hurried down the road toward the schoolhouse. When she reached the door she noticed that it had been tidied up after last night's cakewalk. She opened the windows to let in the fresh morning air. She shuddered, thinking of the plump, straw-haired Harry and his fierce possessive air, and shrugged off the memory. My job is to teach school; every other thought must go, she decided. No doubt, Brad, Ed and Jeremy were on their way northwest.

She shook her head and began to write lesson assignments on the blackboard when the creak of the outside door made her turn. The Culp twins stood in the doorway, alike as two buttons on a Sunday coat.

"Mornin', Miss Tate," one said, and the other echoed, "Miss Tate," although it sounded more like "mistake." The one with the mole is Phenie, she remembered.

"Good morning, Tryphena. And to you, Tryphosa. Would you like to help me pass out the spellers? We'll start with them this morning."

Roxy blew in next, with her usual air of "Well, here I am."

"Folks sure liked you last night," she offered. "Dot like last year's teacher, who allus took it out od the Krebeiers."

Annamarie raised her eyebrow. "Oh? Why was that?"

"They's four of 'em. Don't have nothin' decent to eat or wear," Phenie cut in and

Phosie grunted in response.

"B-But —" Annamarie sputtered. The boiled cabbage, she remembered. It was probably all they had to eat.

The day flew by and soon it was time to sing the "beddidiction." The week flew by, too, and by Thursday she felt better acquainted with most of the pupils and had things under control.

After school she decided to visit the Kremeiers and see for herself what the state of affairs was. It was a short, pleasant walk east. As she approached the farm she noticed the land littered with weeds and broken limbs flanked by a bedraggled field of sunflowers. The yard was equally untidy. A bit of this and a scrap of that, a broken chair and a rusty hoe leaned against the front stoop.

Mrs. Kremeier came to the door at Annamarie's knock. She looked as decrepit as the broken chair on the stoop.

"Oh, it's Teacher. Come in." Her voice was flat and dull as she shoved the chair out of the way with one bare foot.

Inside, the kitchen looked as though a storm had hit it. On the massive black range a sooty water kettle was boiling over next to a bucket of steaming oats. Somewhere in the background wafted the inevitable odor of boiled cabbage. Annamarie nearly choked on the stifling mixture of smells that permeated the room.

"Why don't you set?" Mrs. Kremeier pointed aimlessly toward a chair.

Annamarie would have, if there had been an empty one available. The backless chairs were strewn with old newspapers, dirty towels and empty paper boxes. She stood, hesitating.

Mrs. Kremeier, sensing the situation, languidly pushed the newspaper-towel-box assortment to the floor, and with as little effort as possible shoved the chair toward Annamarie. As she sat down she thought, *I may have to wash my dress as soon as I get home.*

One by one the children straggled in: Mae in her familiar dirty blue dress, followed by Walter, one skinned knee exposed through tattered trousers. Danny yanked up one suspender and held onto the waistband of his pants. The fourth child moved like a shadow in the doorway, then seeing it was the teacher, disappeared quickly.

"What kin I do for you, Teacher?" Mrs. Kremeier said in her colorless voice.

Annamarie swallowed hard. "I noticed the children . . . aren't eating anything at noon except cornbread. They seem to be hungry in the afternoon. Perhaps they need something more, like an apple."

"Don't have apples. Don't have nothin' else, 'cept cabbage. My man's ailin' and can't get the crops in. The young'uns and me, we make a garden. So we do the best we can. The mill grinds our corn for free."

Through the open door she could see Jed Kremeier lounging on a sagging rocker reading a newspaper. Weakly she nodded. He hadn't acknowledged her arrival. She suspected Jed Kremeier was more lazy than "ailin'."

"I'll see if I can bring a sackful of apples from our orchard," she mentioned to Mrs. Kremeier, who gave no reply.

Excusing herself as soon as possible, she got up to leave. "I . . . I feel your children are smart and will do well in school, if fed properly. I pray that somehow you can keep going."

"The boys go possum huntin' on Saturdays. That helps out. And we do raise lots of cabbage in our garden." As the woman opened the door, Annamarie scooted out as quickly as possible.

What can I do to help the Kremeier family? she asked herself as she walked down the dusty road toward the Powers' place.

When she mentioned the situation at suppertime, Ben snorted.

"That Jed Kremeier's the laziest coot in

the county. People know it and that's why no one takes pity on 'em."

"But the poor children —"

"Now and then someone stops by and leaves a jug of milk or some out-growed clothes. The boys is right-minded and when they're old enough they'll prob'ly find work."

"Mrs. Kremeier mentioned the boys shooting possums. Do you suppose they eat them?"

"Sure. Why not? You make do with what you can find."

No wonder she had felt nauseous from the cooking fumes at their house!

Annamarie rode home thoughtfully that Friday afternoon. Most of her students were doing well in school aside from a few problems like the Kremeiers' hunger, Roxy's adenoids, the Culp twins' unflappable actions and Herman Kohfeld's pouty lower lip. At least, her busy schedule kept her from thinking so much about Brad. Thus far Harry hadn't shown up. She'd handle him if he did.

Her mother and Susan were busy with supper preparations when she rode up. They peppered her with questions about her week at school. Even the boarders almost collapsed with laughter as she imitated Roxy's adenoidal twang and the Culp twins' responses.

On Saturday afternoon she went to the store for some buttons and thread to fix her yellow blouse. She had just paid for her purchases when she felt a sharp tug on her arm. As she turned, she saw Linda Corling standing there with every blond curl perfectly in place.

"Oh, Annamarie, I must talk to you!"

Annamarie took a deep breath. "What can I do for you, Linda?" *What does she want with me now that Brad isn't around?* she thought.

The soft piquant features turned to marble. "Why didn't you stop Brad from going to fight the Indians?"

"Why didn't I stop —" Annamarie gasped. "What do you mean, 'Why didn't I stop him?' "

"Brad was so crazy in love with you that all he ever talked about, raved about, was Annie Tate! If you would've told him to stay . . ."

Annamarie didn't hear the rest of Linda's tirade, only the words "All he ever raved about was Annie Tate." *Oh, Brad, Brad,* her heart wept, *so you did care about me! I only wish I'd have known for sure. I'd have been more understanding, more tolerant. I'd have told you goodbye. Now it's too late!*

". . . but you had to play the classy schoolmarm with no time for anyone else!" Linda's harsh words raged on.

"Oh . . ." Annamarie sighed. "I'm sorry, Linda, but I told Brad the decision was his, and that he should ask God for direction. I'm sure that's what he did. I know he'd always cared for me but when you came I was no longer sure."

Linda scowled, "I tried my best to snag him, but he wouldn't budge." She continued more passively, "He said he loves you, although he'd be my friend, and so would you. That's all."

If only I'd known, Annamarie agonized. *And I did promise to be Linda's friend*, she reminded herself.

"Linda, believe me, I'll try to be your friend, if I can. But you'll have to be honest and forthright or it won't work. Friendship works both ways."

Linda nodded. "I guess you're right. But I liked Brad so much and now he's gone."

"We'll have to pray that he'll come back safely."

"I . . . I don't know much about praying, but I'll try, if you say so. By the way, before he went away he said he was leaving a letter in your cave post office."

Annamarie's eyes widened. Perhaps he had more to say in his farewell letter. She'd check it out later.

As she walked up Pine Street a few minutes later, Graham Scott fell into step beside her.

"I trust your teaching's going well, Miss Tate? When you were home last, your enthusiasm was somewhat lacking," he said in his easygoing manner. "I'm sorry you missed seeing off your friends."

"Yes." She nodded slowly. "There was a . . . a misunderstanding between Brad and me, but I think it's cleared up now."

"Such a lovely young lady shouldn't have to worry about her betrothed going to fight Indians. Is something troubling you?"

She felt her face flush. "We weren't . . . betrothed, but there had been a tacit understanding earlier . . . which grew somewhat shaky under the . . . circumstances."

He was silent and thoughtful on the rest of the way to the house, and as soon as she could leave without seeming disrespectful she hurried up the cliff path toward the cave. She was eager to read Brad's letter.

When she reached the cave, she crept inside and felt around their special crevice for the letter, but it felt empty. She reached in deeper. There was nothing. Annamarie drew back with a short sob. Linda must have been lying!

CHAPTER 11

Autumn came, slow and gloomy, with persistent wet mists that slogged down the prairie in watery streams, leaving the atmosphere gray and colorless.

Annamarie stood at the window of her bedroom and watched the rain streak the small panes before leaving to walk to school. She thought of Harry Jensen during his visit last night. His jovial, moon face framed in straw-colored hair was all aglow as he eagerly asked her to go on a moonlight ride. She had refused politely.

"I'm busy with schoolwork, things I must prepare for tomorrow."

"Then I'll ride out to your place next Sunday afternoon. You don't work on school things all the time, do you?"

She smiled weakly. "It all depends upon what my mother's plans are and when I get my clothes washed for the coming week," she said. "I have friends, too, who want to see me when I'm home."

"I have a distinct feeling you don't wanna go with me," he sniffed. "It's time I find me a wife. I've got this farm, see? And I'm building a nice little house. After I finish it, I wanna get married. You'd do just fine."

"I'm sure you'd be a good provider, Harry, but I'm not ready to think of getting married."

"Well, at least, think on it. You and me'd make a good team. I'm not givin' up yet!"

He rode away into the dusk.

When she had mentioned Harry to Emmy Lou, her friend had said wistfully, "My, it must be nice to have all those beaus like you do. No one ever asks me to go riding!"

As she sloshed through the mud to the schoolhouse, her boots oozed with mud at every step in the wagon ruts.

The day at school had gone well, in spite of the rain that had drummed incessantly on the windows. During the noon recess she kept the younger ones busy with seat work, and the older ones working on maps. During singing class, Roxy suggested they sing "My Body Lies over the Ocean." Trying to choke back her laughter, Annamarie let Roxy's loud alto carry the lead, which kept drowning out the "My Bonnies" of the other pupils.

She had decided to visit the Culp home that afternoon. She had gone to visit the pupils in their homes, and now only a few remained. These visits had helped her un-

127

derstand their problems better and made for a more pleasant relationship.

It had rained most of the week, but now the sun shone through thin breaks in the clouds. She decided to ride Lady to the Culps' since they were quite a distance from the Powers and she preferred to ride since the ground was so wet.

Mrs. Culp was a plump, quiet woman who motioned Annamarie into a cozy armchair in the neat Culp kitchen. It was an effort to draw out the mother so Annamarie decided to mention autumn plans. Yes, Mrs. Culp knew Thanksgiving was coming, but she offered little more in the way of conversation. No matter. The twins were more than happy to visit and they liked Miss Tate for a teacher. Each tried to out-do the other in their wisdom, and Annamarie tried to conceal her mirth at times.

"If you'd marry Harry you'd be our cousin. Did you know he's our kin?" Phenie informed her frankly to which Phosie added, "Yes, a truly cousin for a teacher!"

Annamarie pressed her lips together. "But you see, if I'm to be your teacher, I must stay with my job, and not try to be a farmer's wife, too."

Their chatter implied that it wouldn't matter. Harry was used to doing things by himself. She said goodbye when it was almost time for supper and rode back to the Powers'.

Previously she had brought a large sack of apples from the Tate orchard for the Kremeiers and the four "stair steps" had devoured them voraciously.

Autumn plans at school included decorating the classroom during their free time. The children drew leaves and squirrels and made posters for the walls. They even pasted some of them on the windows.

"Our last year's teacher never would'a let us do that," Johnny Case told her brashly. "This covers up the rainy windows, don't it? You make school funner than she did," he concluded, to which there was a clamorous agreement.

Mentally Annamarie reviewed the "rules for students" she had picked up at the Institute earlier:

Respect your teacher.
Obey and accept your punishment.
Do not call your schoolmates names or fight with them.
Don't make noises or disturb your seatmates as they work.
Do not leave your seat without permission.
Be silent during classes . . .

She sighed. Yes, they were good pupils. Somehow she had never felt she could be a good teacher, but apparently they respected and obeyed her. She hadn't expected school to be so enjoyable.

As the days grew shorter she rode home early on Saturday morning instead of late Friday afternoon.

She left at daybreak and arrived in Council Grove at mid-morning on Saturday. Her mother welcomed her with a warm hug, asking her how she'd fared with the rain and mud during the week.

"Oh, the children are so good about helping. They even fight about who's going to sweep the dirty floors. We finally draw straws."

Suddenly she spied a letter from Brad on the table. She tore it open eagerly but her eyes misted as she read it:

September 10, 1868

Dear Annie,

Just wanted to tell you we've trained hard at Fort Harker. Scouts brought news yesterday of another Indian attack on a wagon train 20 miles west, and we're getting ready to go after them. We have our blankets, saddles, bridles, lariats, canteens, butcher knives, tin cups, tin plates, and good Spencer rifles and Colt revolvers, plus plenty of ammunition ready for action. We'll each take seven days' ration of food as we push northwest to look for Indian signs. Col. Forsythe has us fifty volunteers hopping! I'll send this letter along with freighters who travel along the Santa Fe Trail and hope you'll get it somehow. I didn't tell you before I left, Annie, but I love you very much. Please look after Linda. She needs someone. God bless you!

Yours always,
Brad

Annamarie went to her room to lie down after reading the letter. She wept until her pillow was soggy. *Oh, dear Lord, why did I brush him off? Why didn't I tell him goodbye?*

She heard her mother and Susan call to her that they were going out to the store. When she came downstairs, everyone had gone out, so she finished the washing that her mother had started.

That afternoon Linda came over. Annamarie was ironing her freshly washed dresses. As she eased the iron over the ruffles on her green and blue plaid, she sighed. Brad was still on her mind.

"You look sort of peaked, Annamarie," Linda said, fluffing a pillow before plumping herself into a chair near the table where Annamarie was ironing. Annamarie smoothed the full skirt of her pink gingham. "Does teaching do this to you? I thought you liked it. Emmy Lou says you do."

Annamarie drew a deep breath. "Oh, I enjoy my work as a teacher very much even though it's hard. I never knew how satisfying it could be to help twenty school children. You should try it, Linda!"

Linda's pale face looked startled. "Emmy Lou tells me you have a beau out there." She pleated the sash on her hat that was spread out on her lap. "So if teaching's not making you peaked, it must be Brad. You haven't heard from him, have you?"

"Yes. I got a letter he wrote back in September."

"Oh! What did he say? You'll tell me, won't you? He was my friend, too, you know."

Annamarie set down her iron. "The cavalry's out on the Plains now, following the Cheyennes. He —"

"Did he say anything about me?" Linda prodded. "The paper said the boys had reached the Kansas Pacific and were stationed at Fort Harker. They're still there, aren't they?"

"Brad said, . . ." *I won't tell her what Brad said about loving me.* She swallowed before she continued. "He said . . . said I was to look after you, Linda. That you needed someone."

"Did he say . . . anything else . . . about me?"

"No. That was all. But when I think of the boys marching into that terrible menace of the Plains and the enemy they're pursuing, I can hardly bear it. All I can do is pray and pray, and cry, that he will do the job he set out to do, and come back safely."

Linda continued to toy with her sash. "Did you read the letter Brad left for you in that secret post office?" Her voice sounded a little smug.

"No."

"Why didn't you read it?"

Annamarie picked up the iron again and pressed the last ruffle. "Because . . . there wasn't any letter."

Without another word, Linda jumped to her feet and walked over to get her cape. As Mrs. Tate showed her to the door, Annamarie thought, *Now what was all that about? Does Linda know something she isn't telling? What was in Brad's missing letter?*

Shaking her head, she hung up the freshly-ironed dress and pulled at the ruffled flounce. Then she sighed again. *I've tried to be her friend, but it isn't easy. There's something Linda isn't telling me. If only I knew what it was.*

CHAPTER 12

News of the Indian wars had dribbled in from travelers along the Santa Fe Trail, the reports from the army and the Kansas newspapers.

Annamarie cringed when she read what was happening, not knowing whether Brad was in the midst of fighting. She devoured every word of the news.

It seemed the Indian raids had continued all along the Kansas frontier. General Sheridan with 2,600 men under his command had 1,800 who were occupied with protecting forts, railroads and stage lines. The 800 left were not enough to launch a major offensive against the Cheyenne warriors, so he had to rely on volunteers. He had ordered Major General Forsythe to gather fifty men, called scouts, to go after the raiding Indians. Most volunteers were Civil War veterans from both the North and the South and were believed to be some of the best fighting men in the country. Annamarie was sure this was the troop Brad had joined.

After training at Fort Harker they had

gone west to pursue the roving Cheyennes who had split into small groups and scattered over the Plains to hit as many settlements as possible. When the Cheyennes had spotted Forsythe's small troop, they suddenly hemmed them in from the north, the west and the south by swarming toward the tiny army. Forsythe's men took the only way out by escaping to an island in the Arickaree River. But while they fled to the island for safety, the warriors shot their horses one by one. They fortified themselves by digging ditches on the island.

The Indians seemed furious that the scouts had gotten away with their ammunition intact. Then Roman Nose, the six-foot-three-inch Cheyenne chief, recklessly led nearly 300 warriors who hurled charge after charge upon the island. Forsythe's troop fought valiantly, firing volley after volley upon the enemy. On the fifth volley, Roman Nose and his horse fell. This thwarted the reckless fighting and the Cheyennes' charges became half-hearted.

Annamarie shuddered at the news — and the lack of it. It was believed five scouts were dead. Who were they? She groaned in agony. There was no further word.

November winds howled across the Plains and squaw winter came with the early cold spell of autumn and the first honking of wild geese flying in V-shapes to the South.

Big logs crackled in the fireplace of the cozy parlor at the Tate house as Annamarie relaxed after a long, hard week at Clear Ridge. Her thoughts were never far from Brad in following the Indians. Word had finally come that Forsythe's men were saved after two scouts had risked their lives, slipped through enemy lines, and reached Fort Wallace ninety miles away for reinforcements. The men were jubilant when the soldiers from the Fort brought food and horses, and the Indians had finally withdrawn.

But the wars weren't over.

Mrs. Keitch had a letter from her son Ed, which she shared with the town. "Brad Bennett escaped with a slight wound in his shoulder," he wrote. Annamarie wept silently with relief. "But the Indians aren't completely defeated. They've killed over 150 people, including railroad construction workers and fourteen women. Four women and twenty-four children were stolen and eleven stagecoaches attacked. General Sheridan strongly feels a winter campaign is necessary to track the Indians to their winter quarters and force them to their reservation. Brad, Jeremy and I are going with him."

Once more Annamarie felt an overwhelming sense of sadness. Back at Clear Ridge it was hard to hold back the tears as she stood before her students who sensed her preoccupation.

"You look sad, Teacher. Maybe Cousin Harry could cheer you up," Phenie offered, and Phosie added, "Maybe he could."

Annamarie hugged them both. "Thank you for your concern, girls, but I don't think that would do. Tell you what. Let's make turkey and Pilgrim cutouts after recess to put in the windows. You'd like that, wouldn't you?"

Johnny Case beamed. "Maybe I can draw a pitcher of that Massasoit chief, the big Injun what ate with the Pilgrims, ya know."

The mention of the word "Injun" sent a chill through Annamarie. She composed herself quickly and nodded. "That's a great idea. You draw beautifully, Johnny. And yes, he was a good Indian. There are lots of good Indians, of course."

"Like the Kaws," Johnny added, and again Annamarie was reminded of her lost Indian friend, Po-a-be.

But all her efforts at keeping a cheerful front only made the children more restless than they had been all fall.

Roxy seemed to have taken a strong liking to Walter Kremeier for some reason and used all her feminine and not-so-feminine wiles to attract him.

"Walter, Walter, where's your halter?" Johnny teased. "Be careful or Roxy will drag you to the Rock of Gibraltar!"

"Or to the altar!" added Herman, his lip drawn up.

The pupils burst into fits of laughter, and Annamarie tried to quiet them. "Children! Children! Please remember your manners and show your respect!" she said sternly. "Remember that a good pupil is kind."

The days drifted past slowly but to Annamarie they seemed interminable. When she came home on Wednesday afternoon for the Thanksgiving holiday, the Tate kitchen was fragrant with the aromas of pumpkin pies baking and prairie chickens roasting in the oven.

"I decided if I was going to stick my feet under your mother's table for Thanksgiving dinner," Graham Scott explained, taking Annamarie's coat, "I might as well do my share. The four prairie chickens I got were an easy shot," he mentioned casually. "I think Linda Corling expects you to be her guest on Thanksgiving Day," he added. "She's a lucky girl."

Annamarie drew back, startled. "What do you mean? She —"

"To have you for a friend." He winked at her. "I see her roaming down to the draw every now and then. It seems to fascinate her."

To the draw? Annamarie shook her head and went into the kitchen to help her mother with supper.

She dressed carefully for prayer meeting that night. She had combed her thick brown hair and put on her simple blue poplin. She'd missed so many prayer meetings this fall and she hoped she would see Emmy Lou there tonight.

She remembered Brad's first night back from college when Pastor Nash had asked them to sing "Oh for a Closer Walk with God." *Dear Lord, I need You so very much. You know how much I miss him,* she prayed.

Linda waited for her at the door of the Brown Jug, lovely in her brown merino trimmed in narrow bands of fur. Tortoise shell combs gleamed in her pale hair, and she looked more fragile than ever. Annamarie looked around quickly for Emmy Lou. Her friend wasn't there.

"Annamarie!" Linda cried, throwing her arms around her shoulders. "You're coming to our house for Thanksgiving dinner tomorrow, aren't you? You absolutely must!"

Annamarie drew back. "I . . . I'm sorry,

Linda, but my mother's counting on me. I don't see her all week and she has planned a special dinner."

"Oh, you can't mean that!" Linda pouted. "She has all those old boarders and your sister. She won't miss you. I'd so counted on you and I having a really cozy chat. After all, we both have Brad in common."

With a sigh, Annamarie hung up her coat. "But there's no news to share, Linda. He's not here . . . and even if he were —"

"I wonder if he would eat Thanksgiving dinner at your house — or mine?"

Without a word, Annamarie moved to the hall. *If I'm supposed to be her friend, I'll pretend I didn't hear that intimidating comment,* she thought. Then she walked abruptly toward the front and sat down.

Pastor Nash beamed at her and came to shake her hand. "It is good to see you at prayer meeting, Annamarie. But what I hear about Brad and the other Grove boys is indeed alarming."

"I know."

"Still, our God is able. Remember Isaiah 41 says: 'Fear thou not, for I am with thee; be not dismayed, for I am thy God; I will strengthen thee; yea, I will help thee; yea, I will uphold thee with the right hand of my righteousness.' Just cling to those words for the Lord won't fail you!"

I must believe him, and I must believe God, she thought. *In all thy ways acknowledge Him and He shall direct thy paths. . . . Oh, Lord, just help me to trust You more!*

When prayer meeting was over, she started toward the door. Linda was waiting for her, a strange gleam in her green eyes. She grabbed Annamarie's arm.

"I hope you know what you're doing. There's something I had wanted to tell you if you came over tomorrow. But now I won't!" Then she spun around and hurried off.

Annamarie watched her go. What was behind Linda's puzzling words? Did they have anything to do with Brad? *Oh, dear God, I'm more confused than ever!*

CHAPTER 13

December turned raw and cold. Great flocks of ducks flew down from the north, gleaned the last of the grain from the farm fields, then winged their way south. A light snow had fallen and the ice on the small creeks sparkled like opaque glass on the surfaces. The Kaws on Big John Creek pointed out that the beavers were at work. This meant a wet year.

Annamarie plunged into her schoolwork as though it was the goal of every child in her schoolroom to be a star pupil. The big round stove in the center of the room poured out waves of warmth and children huddled as near as they dared.

With Christmas only a scant week away, she worked diligently on their Christmas program. The younger children had woven red-and-green paper chains to hang as streamers across the room while the older ones — especially the girls — cut out stars and covered them with scraps of foil from cigar boxes for the tree.

The Kremeiers held back when Roxy and

the twins chattered about "drawing names" for gifts.

"We don't got the money for that," Walter said bluntly, and Annamarie agreed that to exchange gifts was out of the question.

"How about a grab box then? That way everyone can bring what they can afford," she suggested.

"But is that fair if Mae Kremeier brings a pinecone, and she draws a pretty hair clip?" Phenie grumped. "I don't need any pinecones!"

Annamarie nodded. That posed a question. "Let's forget about a grab box then," she said, realizing that it put a damper in Christmas gift giving at school, although those would probably be the only presents the Kremeiers would receive.

"Our Pa can carve real nice horses from a piece of walnut branch," Danny Kremeier snorted. "We can do somethin'. We ain't that poor!"

If it would provide peace in the school, this could be the answer. It was finally agreed that if Mr. Kremeier would consent to carve nice objects this might be the most logical solution. But would Jed Kremeier get the gifts carved in time?

The night of the program the children came to school dressed in their Sunday best

— all except the Kremeiers, who wore their tattered school clothes. Mae's blue dress showed signs of having been washed recently. Most of them clutched newspaper-wrapped gifts and laid them mysteriously into the grab box Annamarie had decorated with swatches of leftover wallpaper. She silently counted heads to make sure there were enough gifts for the number of children present and placed it under the lopsided evergreen. The tree shone with the aluminum-covered stars as candles flickered on the scrawny branches. The room soon bulged with parents in the dim lantern light as pupils seated themselves cross-legged on the floor in front of the room until Annamarie announced it was time to sing.

Then forty restless feet scraped the floor like a herd of buffalo crossing the prairie as they faced the crowd. Twenty gusty voices shrilled the great Christmas carols as Annamarie shook her head.

"O come lettuce adore Him, O come lettuce adore Him . . ."

She had shoved encouragement down the raspy throats for two weeks and she was tired. The performance didn't sound nearly as good as the practice. If only the program was over.

Walter Kremeier's shoe flapped persistently as he tapped his foot to the beat of each Christmas carol causing a few grown-up snickers. Roxy did an admirable job of reciting "The Three Wise Men," if the audience didn't mind her referring to them as the "wise bed."

Annamarie was relieved when the program finally ended, and the children grabbed a gift from the grab box. Jed Kremeier had come through with beautifully carved horses and the children who drew the gifts were the envy of the entire school.

As the last straggler, clutching a sack of candy and nuts, finally left with a cheery, "Merry Christmas, Miss Tate," Annamarie heaved a sigh of relief. She was alone at last. Now to douse the fire, snuff the candles and lanterns and collect her small pile of gifts from the children including a perky hair bow from Roxy and a pair of identical pink handkerchiefs from the Culp twins.

Then she heard, "Annamarie!"

Turning, she saw Harry Jensen in front of her, his straw-colored hair awry, with a plump arm behind him, grinning like a house cat. Then slowly he held out one pudgy hand clutching a tiny box.

"Here. It's for you!"

Annamarie's eyes widened. "What . . . what is it, Harry?"

146

"Open it and see." He laid the box in her hand.

As she opened it, a shiny gold necklace glittered in its bed of cotton. He nodded, then placed his hands on his hips his eyes sparkling.

"It was so purty, I wanted you to have it. For Christmas."

"But Harry —"

"I had a good fall crop and when I was down to Topeka a few weeks ago, I saw it. I knew I had to get it for you."

"It's beautiful. But Harry," she sputtered, "I can't accept it. Not that I don't appreciate it, but it wouldn't be fair to you."

The smile died on his face. "Why not? I've told you more'n once that you suit me just fine. Why can't you take it?"

"Because . . . because I already have a . . . a sweetheart."

"Where is he?" He drew back, startled. "I've never seen him around."

"Harry," her voice was low. "He . . . he's on the plains fighting the Cheyennes. When he returns —"

"Oh, but you know how chancy that is. Them Cheyennes is nasty-bad. If he gets an arrer in his back — pouff! That's it. That's the end of him!"

Annamarie laid the box back in Harry's

hand. Then she backed away.

"You're a very nice young man, Harry, and you deserve a good wife. I'm sorry. But I know I'm not the one for you. You'll find the right girl somewhere, I'm sure."

His gaze held a note of sadness. "But I liked you so much. You love God — I know that. You're a fun person, and that's what I want in a wife!"

"Surely there are other Christian girls."

He looked at her eagerly, as hope burned in his eyes. "Would you . . . do you know of a girl I could visit in Council Grove? You know, I'd be good to her."

Emmy Lou!

"Harry, I have a very close friend who's a jewel and a very faithful Christian. But she's a town girl, and I don't know —"

"Wait 'til she sees my place! What's she look like? Is she purty?"

Annamarie pondered a moment. "Well, she has brown hair and freckles. And she has a delightful smile. She's a hard worker, but she's also full of fun."

"Kin I come up and see her one of these days?"

"Her name's Emmy Lou Hanks, and when I go home in the morning I'll ask her."

With a snappy salute, he whirled around. "Tell her I'll be by the day after Christmas."

Then he hurried out with a bounce in his step.

Annamarie came home the next morning to the aroma of popcorn popping in the iron pan and the bubbling of fudge in a pan.

"M-m-m. Something smells good," she greeted Susan who stood in front of the stove.

"My birthday's tomorrow." She looked up, her face flushed from the heat. "I thought a panful of popcorn and a plate of candy would taste good around the fire. Will you stir the fudge for me, please, while I finish the popcorn?"

"It's hard to believe you're going to be thirteen, Susan," Annamarie said as she stirred the bubbling fudge. "We'll celebrate tomorrow. I'd almost forgotten you were born on Christmas Day. Will the boarders be here on Christmas Day?"

"They asked if they could — all except Mr. Nichols who's going home."

"Where's Mother?"

"She's down at the store for a few things."

"What's for Christmas dinner?"

Susan paused to pour the popped corn into a large bowl. "Oh, someone brought us some venison. I think it was Emmy Lou's father. He shot a deer the other day."

Annamarie drew a deep breath, thinking of Harry's interest in Emmy Lou. Would her friend be as excited as he seemed to be?

"Any news from the boys on the Plains?"

"I think Mr. Johnson may know something. He keeps in touch with Topeka."

"Here. I'll finish that batch," said Susan as she reached for the spoon Annamarie was holding.

Annamarie wondered about Linda. *I should really run up to see her,* she decided. Then she noticed the large plate of fudge cut neatly in cubes.

"May I snatch a plateful of fudge?" she asked, picking up a crumb that had fallen on the table. "You know, this is very good!"

"Is it for Emmy Lou?"

Licking her fingers, Annamarie shook her head. "No, she'll be here tomorrow. I thought I'd bring some to Linda Corling."

She heard Susan draw a deep breath. "Well, I guess you can take some. But I don't really like that snooty Linda very much. She wanted to take Brad away from you!"

"Well, she won't. Brad loves me." She pulled on her wrap and headed for the door. "I'll be back soon."

Letting herself out into the brisk morning air, Annamarie balanced the plateful of fudge on one hand as she scurried down the street.

The streets were full of buggies and wagons. Familiar stores were busy as settlers took care of errands before the holiday.

When she reached the prestigious Corling house, she tried to prepare herself for the visit to Linda.

Walking up the freshly swept gray steps, she knocked on the door. Linda opened the door, every pale hair perfectly in place, and drew Annamarie inside.

The gracious parlor was decorated with pine boughs and sprigs of mistletoe and red roping swung above the windows. The tree in one corner glittered with gay ornaments and glistened with gold and silver trinkets. The pump organ held an array of tall red candles.

"Oh, what a beautiful room!" she exclaimed as she handed the plate to Linda's mother who took her wrap and left the room. "I wanted to bring you a plateful of Susan's fudge. And I wanted to see how you are doing."

"I'm glad you came. This weather's hard on me," she said with a breathless laugh.

It seemed Linda looked more fragile and pale than ever, and she noticed the shaking hands. Was the girl ill? Or did she miss Brad that much?

"You look tired, Linda. Are you all right?"

"As I said before, it's the weather. It hardly seems like Christmas, with so many of the young people gone. I can't even have a party. Here, sit down." Linda motioned Annamarie to a chair and sat across from her.

"Where are the Dillon girls? And the Matthews sisters? And the Stenger boys? Surely some are around?"

Linda shook her head. "Most have gone either to Topeka or to Emporia for the holidays. I didn't want to leave, in case there was word from Brad . . . and the others."

"Then there's been no word?"

"Not since November. They're out on some maneuvers. That's all anyone knows! Oh, Annamarie . . . what's going to happen?" Tears spilled from her green eyes on the white cheeks. "Aren't you worried?"

Was she worried? Of course, she was. But she had tried to commit everything to the Lord. In His time He would answer. She had to believe that.

Leaving the elegant Corling home as soon as she could, she hurried home. Her mother was stirring the fire in the grate and mixing up a panful of biscuits. Venison stew bubbled on the back of the stove, and Annamarie tied an apron around her waist and set the table.

Sara Tate seemed more at ease than she

was the last time Annamarie was home. Annamarie shared the news of Harry's promised visit to Emmy Lou and they laughed over the improbable romance.

"Did you have a good program last night?" Mrs. Tate asked, slicing a loaf of freshly baked wheat bread.

"The practice was better than the performance," she chuckled, "but the older children remembered most of the words to the Christmas carols. We even had a little tree in the classroom."

"Oh, Graham's bringing a tree from the timber," Mrs. Tate reminded herself. "Better get a bucket of water ready to set it in."

Late in the afternoon Graham Scott stomped in with a tall and fragrant tree and set it in the bucket near the window. The girls decorated it with a few simple baubles Susan had made along with a box of older ornaments from years gone by. Editor Johnson said he was contacting Topeka on Christmas Day for more news about the Indian wars.

"Be sure to hang up your stockings tonight, girls. Your gifts are small but I did manage to get something for you, thanks to your salary, Annamarie. We'll do what we can to celebrate the birth of Christ, and Susan's birthday too."

Christmas dawned brittle-cold and clear, and the roads were frozen solid. The warmth of cozy talk around a table filled with plates of roasted venison, mashed potatoes and bowls of stewed dried corn were a welcome meal. Dried apple and custard pies baked by Annamarie topped off the Christmas dinner. It was a pleasant, relaxing time.

The stockings yielded pincushions, freshly hemmed handkerchiefs and fresh-baked ginger cookies. Susan was excused from helping with the work.

After the meal and the dishes were cleared away, Johnson left for his newspaper office. Graham suggested they sing carols and led out. His voice was deep and rich, blending with Annamarie's clear soprano. His reminded her of Brad's strong bass.

"This is a thrice-blest day," Graham announced. "Not only Christmas Day and Susan's birthday, but also the warm time of fellowship with friends." His gray eyes twinkled as he looked at Annamarie, and she turned away quickly.

Minutes later Johnson stepped in, a quiet look on his pensive face. "There was a telegram. General Custer has headed toward Black Kettle's camp on the Washita in Oklahoma Territory. It's believed this will mean less Indian trouble, since they're tracking the

Cheyennes to their winter quarters. The Indian wars may soon be over."

A surge of hope stirred Annamarie's heart. If this were true, Brad would soon be home! Dear Lord, thank You for this news!

CHAPTER 14

January 1869 was held in the grip of winter. A storm broke on New Year's Day and lashed itself into a two-day frenzy before it wore itself out. Snow lay in ridges along the roads and there was the constant thump of the shovel as Ben cleared the way to the barns in an endless fight to care for the stock.

Annamarie bundled up in coats and scarves and donned heavy boots as she pushed her way to the schoolhouse. Ice-winged prairie chickens sat on rail fences in the snow along the road.

She was happier than she'd been in weeks because the winter campaign on the Plains seemed to be going well. Surely the Indians would be subdued before long, and Brad would return.

The pupils arrived late because of the weather, stomping off the snow as they barreled indoors with shouts of laughter. Roxy wore a fine new red coat of which she was justly proud.

"Oh, Biss Tate," she bubbled. "It's good to be back at school. I wuddered if you are going to barry Harry?"

With a thinly-disguised chuckle she said, "Of course, I'm not going to marry him. He's got another girl and seems very fond of her. I think she likes him, too."

"Does it bake you feel sad or glad?"

"Oh, it makes me glad. I'm delighted Emmy Lou's found a nice young man in Harry Jensen."

"Then you'll stay here at Clear Ridge and teach forever?" Phenie put in, unwinding a long red knitted scarf from her neck. Phosie unwound an identical *blue* scarf.

"As long as I can," Annamarie murmured with a quiet smile. "Now let's take our seats. It's time for the bell."

The day went well in spite of the heavy snow drifts beyond the windows. The prairie lay white and still as a dead man in his shroud. Rabbits bounced from the roadsides as they hopped over the snowbanks.

Feeble yellow sunlight filtered through the gray clouds and when the sun came out the outdoors turned into a splendor of dazzling brilliance.

During the noon recess the children bundled up and bounded outdoors for a rousing game of "Fox and Geese." Annamarie stood at the window, watching the exuberant activity in the snow.

Wet mittens and soggy jackets were soon scattered on benches in the schoolroom after she rang the bell. It was time to get back to work. Before long there was only the scritch-scratch of writing on twenty slates.

As she handed out seatwork, Herman Kohfeld sat with his lower lip hanging down again. She felt like shoving it up. The assignment was to write essays.

"Anything wrong, Herman?"

He shrugged his shoulders. "I ain't in no mood to write no essay."

"Why not? The others are doing theirs. I'd like you to show what you can do. Just write about something you know."

Johnny Case, his freckles standing out like bunches of gravel, flapped his hand.

"I wrote mine, Teacher!" he burst out. "Come look at it."

She walked to Johnny's seat and glanced at his slate. He had written:

Making Mony
Mony is made by the U.S. Govermint in big factry's all over the Untied States —

She stifled her laughter at the "Untied States," and patted his shoulder. "You're doing fine, Johnny. Remember to check for spelling errors."

By this time Herman had hauled up his lip and pegged away, letter by letter, word by word on his slate, working diligently.

All too soon school was over for the day. As the benediction was sung, the shuffle of prancing horses and shouts of greeting could be heard as fathers came for their children in farm wagons.

After several happy, sticky goodbyes and the creaking of wagons going down the roads, the schoolhouse was strangely quiet. Somehow she had come to love each of her pupils.

She was grateful for her job. Her salary had helped her mother pay expenses and make payments on the house, so she knew her work was important to Clear Ridge and to her family. The three boarders took up much of the time they had once enjoyed as a family. She missed the familiar togetherness with her mother and sister during the week while she was away and often had to share it when she was home.

As she packed to go home Saturday morning for the weekend, she could hardly wait to hear about Brad and his friends. Surely someone would have heard.

The sun had thawed some of the drifts, and the soft snow spattered under Lady's hooves as she started down the road toward home. She continued down the trail that had led through the north prairie. Already the trunks of the cottonwoods and beeches were black with moisture on their north sides, and the ice on the creeks was turning a dusty gray. In her anxious hurry she nudged Lady a bit faster.

Dead leaves from the rattling branches above blew into the water and floated with a slow, rocking motion in the wind. Out here alone, with only the leafless trees and the brackish water, she could talk to the Lord. She thought of Linda with the pale hair and white face and the obvious pain she had sensed, and she stifled the sudden stab of fear.

"Lord, I've trusted You to care for Brad," she prayed. "But I also feel suddenly disturbed about Linda Corling. Somehow, I've been able to place Brad in Your hands. But I ask for grace and strength for whatever happens. Yet, what about Linda?"

As she rode, she traced the path that her love for Brad had taken. She had cared for him from the first day they had met as children. Their first youthful admiration had grown into something deeper and had survived the past several months while Linda was an obstacle in the path. She realized now that she had claimed him for herself without letting him know.

She sighed. What would Linda do about it? She winced. What *could* she do? Nothing, now that Brad had made it clear he loved Annamarie. All she needed was to know that Brad was coming home.

When she arrived at the house on Pine Street she stabled Lady in the barn and hurried through the back door. The kitchen was deserted. Only a small fire snapped and crackled in the range and sent out feeble thrusts of warmth.

Dropping her valise into the hall, she called out, "Mother? I'm home!"

Hearing voices in the parlor she moved quickly to the neat, freshly cleaned room. The voices stopped when she stepped into the doorway.

A small circle of four persons sat on straight-backed chairs, their faces solemn. Her mother, Susan, Graham Scott and Ed Keitch. They turned as one to look at her but no one spoke.

"Mother? Susan?" Her voice was as frozen as the ground outside. "Is something wrong?"

Ed opened his mouth and closed it again. Then he got up slowly and came toward her, took her arm and led her to a chair.

"Annamarie, I just got back . . . both

Jeremy and I . . . and came here to tell you in person."

"Tell me . . . what?" her words choked in her throat.

He glared somberly at Mrs. Tate and shook his head.

"Tell me what?" she cried again, her words harsh and fearful.

Graham Scott cleared his throat and he half rose to his feet. "Annamarie, Brad is . . . is dead."

"Brad!" she shrieked. "No! I don't believe it! Not after —"

"I'm sorry, Annamarie, but it was so hard for me to tell you," Ed said.

She clenched her fists and beat them on the arms of the chair as her mind raged, *It isn't true. It can't be true! Ed Keitch has made it up. There's no way —*

"Let me tell you what happened," Ed spoke in a low, sad voice, standing beside her with one hand on her shoulder.

She beat her fingers on her lap. "No . . . no, it isn't true, Ed. I'd have known if it were true!"

"Please listen to me, and let me tell you what happened."

"But how do you know, Ed? You're just trying to hurt me. I won't believe —"

"Annamarie, I was there! I saw it happen!"

He paused to take a deep breath. "It was in December when we were with Custer. We left in a fierce blizzard and rode into Indian country, toward the Cheyenne camp along the Washita. The way they had made raids all over Kansas in the fall, General Sheridan decided we needed to investigate some deserted Indian villages in the Washita Valley. We knew that's where the Indians had gone. Brad and I came upon the frozen body of a white woman. We knew what that meant."

Annamarie turned pale. She knew it meant that Cheyennes had been on the rampage and had stolen white captives and killed without mercy. No doubt, the captain had ordered them to find the Indians responsible.

"Go on," she whispered, ice in her veins.

"Indians were hiding in the rocky bluffs along the river, and they surprised us, shooting at us before we got a chance to track them. Then we saw Po-a-be."

"Po-a-be!" Annamarie cried out.

"Brad ran after her. She was running. But one Cheyenne had slipped behind Brad and began to shoot. I saw Brad fall with a cry, clutching his shoulder, his face contorted with pain as he fell. Po-a-be was gone. Behind us more Indians were coming and Jeremy and I knew we couldn't go back so we managed to escape. Later we asked for permission to see if there was anything we could do. When we returned, we saw Brad had been dragged away. Later when we caught up with our division, our captain told us to go home. New troops were to be sent out to wipe up the mess."

Annamarie's voice quivered as she asked, "Are you sure Brad was dead?"

"I'm so sorry, Annamarie. If there's anything I can do."

She shook her head stonily. "Nothing . . . any more. You've done enough."

"I'm so sorry. But he gave you a message. The night before, Brad and Jeremy and I had a long talk in the shelter of a boulder. He said if anything happened to him, he was ready to meet his Savior. And that he loved you more than anything. As for Linda, you should ask her what had been between them."

Annamarie heard Ed's words as from a far distance. It didn't make sense. People cried when dear ones died, but she couldn't cry. Besides, what good would it do? What good were tears now? No amount of weeping could bring him back. Hastily she got up, picked up her wrap and hurried outdoors. She needed to escape from the horrible news.

Her boots scooped up the cold, slushy snow that lay thick on the streets as she slowly walked along. Then she paused. For a while she stood there, staring at a display in a storefront window, crushed, trying to submit to God's will that this had happened. Suddenly she thought of what might have been if Brad had lived to come home. She threw off her meek spirit and hurriedly walked toward the draw. *I had trusted God to keep Brad.*

"God . . . God . . . God!" she groaned out loud as soon as she was away from the town. "All my faith and my prayers can't accomplish one thing now," she raged. "You didn't care. All my tears were in vain."

Nothing but hollow silence greeted her. She sank, weeping, to the frozen ground, her anger spent at last like a great summer storm which passes, sweeping the prairies clean of dust and dirt, but leaving it beaten and very still.

Then she got slowly to her feet, dried her tear-soaked face and brushed the snow off her wrap. She turned back toward the town.

I must be the one to tell Linda, she told herself without enthusiasm. *She'll die a thousand deaths when I do, and she'll blame me for not stopping Brad from leaving. But I must tell her. How shall I tell her? In the kindest way possible. What had Ed meant about Linda telling me something of their past?*

Then the thought hit her: *Neither Linda nor I will have any more claims on Brad.* It went through her like a knife.

She swung around and started walking toward the Corling house.

CHAPTER 15

With her spirit crushed, Annamarie plodded along the edge of the orchard. The trunks of the apple trees were moist and oozing with sap. Puddles had frozen again. *Like me,* she decided. *Maybe the frozen ice of my mind will melt some day.* She would have to face the facts. Yes, but how can one pick out facts when they're intertwined with emotions?

Just when life had finally seemed to be worth living again, she received the sad news. She had thought that since he had declared his love for her, she could wait and pray for Brad's return from reclaiming the vast prairie lands for the settlers. Now Death had closed the door to her dreams and here she was on her way to tell Linda the news, and probably to hear her censure because of it. There was only a deep, hollow throbbing where her heart had been.

Lord, I can't bear this unless You help me, she whispered as she turned down the tree-lined avenue where the Corlings lived. With a firm lift of her chin she marched up the gray steps and rang the bell, then stepped back to wait for someone to open the door.

It creaked for a moment, then opened wide. Linda's pale chiseled prettiness stood before her, her green eyes lit with surprise.

"Oh, it's you, Annamarie. You wanted to see me?" She held open the door and Annamarie stepped into the wide hall, drawing off her long woolen scarf.

"Please come into the parlor," Linda said. "Let's move close to the fire. Isn't it cold outdoors? I can't handle the cold very well, you know."

"Of course."

Annamarie followed Linda to a mulberry-covered easy chair and sat down, grateful for the dimness of the late afternoon light so that Linda wouldn't read the traces of sorrow in her face.

"I suppose your school is going well?"

Nodding Annamarie drummed her fingers on her blue-plaid lap. "Yes, the pupils are doing well, and this snow makes for many a tumble outside. I hope no one comes down with a cold."

"I'm always fearful of people coughing, spreading sickness and all," Linda said petulantly, stretching out her hands before the fire. "It's one of the worse facets of winter!"

"I'm sorry it's so hard on you," Annamarie said politely, trying to make conversation. "I like the snowy prairies." *Why can't I just come out and tell her Brad's dead,* she thought.

"Yes, they are pretty sometimes. Have you . . . any word from Brad yet?" Linda spoke hesitantly. "I know we both look forward to his coming back soon."

"Yes, there's word. Jeremy and Ed are home."

Alarm crossed Linda's face like a spasm. "But, what of Brad? They were together, weren't they? Surely he's coming too?" She clenched her dainty little fists. "Please tell me he's home!"

Annamarie moistened her dry lips. "Linda, Brad . . . Brad was killed by Indians several months ago."

A look of anguish crossed the pale features. "No!" Her delicate face whitened. "It's not true! I won't believe it!"

"It is true, Linda. I didn't want to believe it either. But the boys saw Po-a-be, and Brad rushed out to save her."

"Killed — for one filthy squaw!" Linda's lips curled with scorn. Then she slumped back in her chair, her body limp and her face drawn.

Annamarie suddenly realized Linda had fainted. She jumped up and grabbed Linda's arm and shouted, "Mrs. Corling! Mrs. Corling!"

The regal woman rushed into the room, then pushed Annamarie rudely aside, her face contorted with anger.

"What have you done to my child?" she demanded hoarsely. "You've caused her grief ever since we came to Council Grove!"

Annamarie drew back in amazement. "I . . . caused her grief? That's not true."

The woman wasn't listening. She was chafing the thin white wrists vigorously as she raised her voice sharply. "Mary! Go for the doctor immediately."

The maid scurried from the kitchen and grabbed her coat from the hall. "Yes ma'am. Right away," she said and slammed out of the house.

Mrs. Corling whirled on Annamarie and snapped, "What did you tell my daughter to make this happen? Don't you know she's —" She closed her lips tight.

Startled, Annamarie's eyes grew wide. What was the mysterious malady that seemed to grip Linda Corling in this vacuum?

"Mrs. Corling, what's wrong with Linda? She's sick, isn't she?" she asked.

"Yes, and it's all your fault. If you hadn't taken Brad away from her —"

"But I never took . . . Mrs. Corling, Brad and I have cared for each other for years," she began to explain.

Just then the door burst open and the maid and Dr. Bradford rushed into the room. The short, balding doctor ran toward Linda's side, knelt down and felt the thin wrist. The maid hurried out for a glass of water.

Bowing her head, Annamarie stood quietly as worried thoughts raced and tumbled through her mind. *What is wrong with Linda? What is the answer to this strange situation? Dear Lord, this isn't my doing!* she prayed. *Please let Linda come out of this . . . this stupor! Surely the girl's mother doesn't blame me!*

Dr. Bradford lifted the glass to Linda's lips, and after a few struggling gulps, the girl drank. Annamarie watched Linda closely, then saw the pale eyelids flutter, Linda opened her eyes.

"Anna . . . marie, please tell me . . . that you were only trying to . . . to frighten me. Brad isn't really d-dead?" Her words were a ragged whisper.

Annamarie nodded. "Yes, Linda, he is." She paused to look at Mrs. Corling to see if she should go on, but received no response, so she continued. "According to Ed, the boys were with General Custer in the Washita Valley when their small division was ordered to go after a renegade band of Cheyennes who caught them by surprise. That's when they saw Po-a-be. Ed and Jeremy barely escaped. Brad was . . . shot from behind."

Linda's face was as white as death, and her hands trembled violently. She fought to speak and finally gulped out a few harsh words.

"Are you sure? There was no mistake?"

"That's what Ed Keitch said. I'm sure you're very upset, for it's shaken me up like nothing ever has before. And my father's death was so hard, too, if it weren't for God's everlasting arms underneath."

She sat down. Dr. Bradford spoke a few low words to Mrs. Corling, picked up his bag and left.

"And all for one of those blasted Indians! And don't speak to me of God!" Linda spat out. "Everyone was so sure that the Cheyennes were almost licked, that Brad would come back soon. You even convinced me of it." She shook her head. "If you'd kept him from leaving, he wouldn't have been out fighting Indians. *You* could've kept him from going, but you didn't!"

"I couldn't . . . because he's his own person and I told him to follow his conscience. What else could I do? I love him so much! Don't you think I'm crushed?" she flung out. "And why couldn't *you* persuade him to stay?"

Linda's eyes lowered and she stared down at her shaking hands. "Because . . . because he wouldn't listen. He said he'd do whatever you'd tell him. You could've told him to stay, but you wouldn't!"

"No, Linda, I told him to listen to the Lord. He was obedient to His leading." She got to her feet. "I'm very tired and very grieved. I need to be alone and pray. I'm sorry I had to hurt you and bring you this sad news, but you had to hear it."

"I only wish —"

"Linda, Ed said the boys had talked seriously for a long time one night about home and their plans for the future. Brad had said if anything happened to him you would tell me what there had been between you. Now is the time. What was it, Linda?"

The girl shook her head stonily. "Go away! Not now! I can't talk about it now!"

Slowly Annamarie wound her scarf around her head, and with a compassionate glance at the blond girl, she let herself out the door. It was easy to see the heartbreak on Linda's face, but her own spirit was bruised and battered, too. She dragged her weary body down the street toward home rubbing her mittened hands together against the cold which she scarcely felt. It didn't seem possible. Brad, strong and stalwart with a man's physique and a man's spirit, crumpled to the ground from an Indian's bullet. The breeze had grown chilly after the rather mild day and blew her hair back from her forehead. She heard footsteps behind her. Then the familiar creased face of Pastor Nash beamed at her as he gently touched her arm.

"Annamarie, I just heard," he said quietly. "I understand your deep sorrow. I only wish I could bring him back. But —" He shook his gray head.

"Oh, why did it have to happen when the fight was going so well against the Cheyennes!" she wailed.

"I know it's hard to understand. Although we're so prone to forget that God is in control, He has a reason for everything!"

"But to snatch the life of a promising young man like Brad, I can't understand."

"Yes, I know. Just remember, God created the red man, too. So perhaps there's a double purpose behind all of this."

Annamarie shook her head slowly. What reason could God have? It didn't make sense, no matter what the pastor said. How could this be the will of God? Brad hadn't been able to save Po-a-be after all.

Pastor Nash paused. As they stood together in the brittle afternoon, he added, "I want to share with you one of the conversations I had with Brad once. He said, 'Pastor Nash, whether I live or whether I die, I am the Lord's.' He looked upon his life as something God had given to him to use. He knew Jesus had died for his sins, and thus, he could lay claim to the mercy of God."

"But he tried to rescue Po-a-be! Surely this was in God's plan!" she cried.

They had reached the corner of Pine Street and stopped. He took her outstretched hand and shook it warmly.

"Thank you, Pastor Nash. That's exactly how I knew Brad, too. But for awhile he seemed taken by Linda Corling and it hurt me so. I'm sure at the time he had a good reason for it, but at that time it upset me very much because I couldn't understand. Yet to know he died trying to save my Indian friend —"

"Brad loved you. There was never a doubt in my mind. Whatever he did for Linda, he had his reasons. You may never learn what they were." He tipped his hat and walked toward the Brown Jug. "Goodbye, my dear," he called out over his shoulder. "May God comfort and strengthen you!"

For a long time Annamarie stood on the corner until dusk began to lean down slowly. She thought of the pastor's words. Although she was trying hard to understand, she recalled Linda's harsh words, "Don't speak to me of God!" and shook her head gravely. The poor girl didn't have God's strength and His grace to lean on, and a stab of pity knifed through her.

She hurried to the Tate house and stood on the porch. She knew her mother was worried when she'd walked out of the house earlier. *I do have the Comforter,* she told herself. It was more than Linda had.

"Annamarie?" her mother called out from the kitchen. "I was concerned when you left so abruptly. Did you see Linda?"

"Yes." She nodded. "She's taking it so hard, Mother — although I'm sure she knew Brad loved me. But I'm sure she doesn't know our loving Savior, which makes it harder for her."

"Some day she will." Mrs. Tate scraped potatoes into a blue bowl at the table. "You know the Source of strength."

"Yes, Mother, and I'm glad for that. Yet it's so hard . . ."

Graham Scott came into the room and paused at Annamarie's side. His craggy face was filled with compassion. Looking at her curiously, he said, "The news about Brad must've been devastating. The whole town is shaken up. You will survive this, my dear. I'm praying for you."

She turned tear-filled eyes to his. "Thank you, Graham. It means a lot to me. It means a lot to me," she repeated.

He took her hand and pressed it gently, almost too firmly, and she grimaced.

CHAPTER 16

For Annamarie the next two days dragged by. On Sunday afternoon as she sat before the fire, the cold February winds had whooped from the north. They had banged and shook and thumped all morning. But now they sounded like harps in the bare trees swept by fingers of rain and wind.

Harps. Brad loved the Lord and now he was among those who sang praises to the Lord in the starry heavens. She shook her head, still not ready to believe he was gone. How could she go on, knowing he would never come back? Still, what made it more bearable was the fact that he tried to save Po-a-be's life. She prayed that her friend had escaped — some way.

A sudden idea hit her and she jumped up and ran upstairs. "Graham! Graham!" she called out as she rapped on the door of his room. "Are you in there?"

As he opened the door his blond hair was tousled and his shirt rumpled. A wry grin crossed his face.

"You woke me up from my nap just in

time! I guess this brisk weather makes one sleepy. I slept for a good hour. What can I do for you, my dear?"

Annamarie drew back sharply, an embarrassed flush on her cheeks. She hoped the term "my dear" had slipped out unintentionally.

"I just happened to think. Running Elk should know Po-a-be's still alive. I don't know if he could do anything about finding her, but if you'd tell him . . ."

"Please set your mind at ease, Annamarie," he said. "I told him right away when I realized the boys had seen her in the Washita River Valley. He's on his way with several other warriors right now to look for her."

She beamed. "You're very perceptive, Graham, and I should've realized you'd tell our Kaw friends as soon as you knew."

"Yes, I didn't dare waste much time. He was so glad I told him. I'm not assistant Indian agent for nothing! He loved her, you know."

I'd wondered about that, Annamarie thought. *I only hope he finds her. When he does, maybe she can tell us more about Brad.* She caught Graham's lingering gaze on her face, and she jerked her head away quickly. Then he excused himself and went back to his room.

She went to the bedroom she shared with Susan and packed her small valise and donned her heaviest wraps. It was time to head back to Clear Ridge, in spite of the deep chill outdoors.

Mrs. Tate retied Annamarie's shawl snugly and gave her a warm hug. "It's dreadfully unpleasant outdoors for your ride back," she said as she held the door open. "How I wish you didn't feel you had to teach school to help out with family finances."

"But I want to, Mother. Yes, and I do love all my twenty pupils, from Roxy's adenoids to the Kremeiers' cabbage!"

"Will you go back for the fall term?"

Annamarie cocked her head. "I haven't fully decided, Mother. If it will keep you and Susan more comfortable, I shall. Yet somehow the Lord hasn't given me peace about promising for another term. I'm still praying about it." She looked at the Seth Thomas clock on the wall. "It's time to saddle Lady and get on the road. It gets dark soon these chilly winter days." *The ice in my heart is still there,* she thought.

After her goodbyes to her mother and Susan, she led Lady from her stall and climbed on her back. The cold wind bit sharply through her clothes as they headed down the frozen trail, and she drew her wraps snugly around her.

She was glad that Running Elk had set out to find Po-a-be. Although Brad was lost to her, she hoped her Indian friend was still alive.

Editor Johnson had printed more news in the last issue of the *Advertiser*. The other tribes, after overwhelming delays, he wrote, had finally been subdued — all except the Cheyennes, who, with tricks and lies, had managed to elude the armed forces and escaped to the southwest. Chiefs Satanta and Lone Wolf of the Kiowas were held as hostages. It was due to General Custer's diplomatic handling that they had captured the remaining Plains Indians and herded them to their reservations. The captive chiefs were well clothed and well fed in a comfortable lodge at Fort Sill.

Some Eastern papers, wrote Johnson, knew little of the raging battles and the situations and had lauded Satanta as a hero. Black Kettle, whom Custer had slain, was considered a martyr. The Eastern editors urged that the extreme penalty of the civil law be meted out to Custer and Sheridan in particular, not to mention to the rest of the Kansas cavalry.

It was good to know that most of the fighting was over and only mopping up was still ahead. But what a price it had taken to buy this freedom for the settlers on the prairies!

The chill had seeped into Annamarie's body and her hands and feet felt like chunks of ice by the time she rode into the Powers' yard. Ben jumped from the kitchen door, bundled in his heavy duckcoat as he helped her from the horse and carried her valise indoors. Then he went to stable Lady.

Lizzie hopped from her rocker when Annamarie came in and gave her a hearty hug. "Sakes, child, you must be frozen stiff! I should'a insisted you stay here for the weekend. No need to ride back home in this winter chill."

Annamarie held her hands to the fire. "Thank you, Lizzie. I appreciate your concern, but I want to see my mother at least on weekends, whenever I can."

"Too bad you don't have a gentleman friend what could drive you over in some carriage. Or at least a buggy. Maybe you could make up with Harry again."

A spasm of pain crossed Annamarie's face and she shook her head. "I told Harry earlier that I wasn't interested — even if Brad is — gone."

"Well, what about that feller Scott what helps the Kaw agent? Don't you reckon he coulda drove you up here?"

"Graham?" Annamarie smiled. "He's one of my mother's boarders and a good friend, that's all."

Just then Ben stomped into the kitchen and drew off his wraps, beating his hands together.

"Sure's tarnation cold out there. I'm s'prised you wasn't froze. Sure hope that Injun fightin' is over for good on the Plains. Wonder whatever happened to them young fellers what stopped by on the night of the cakewalk before they left to fight." He pulled out a chair near the stove and slumped into it.

"Ed and Jeremy have returned. They — they say the worst of the fighting is over. But the Cheyennes have fled." She paused and sighed.

"What of the feller who wanted to tell you goodbye that night?"

Lizzie was puttering with food at the table, stirring a panful of turnips and slicing crusty chunks of bread.

Annamarie's heart gave a lurch. "Oh — Brad — Brad was killed, trying to save an Indian girl."

"An Injun gal?" Ben exploded. "But I thought that's who they was fightin'. He sure didn't show much sense."

"She is from the Kaw reservation near us

183

and was kidnapped by the Cheyennes last June. In trying to rescue her, Brad got a bullet in his back."

Both Ben and Lizzie grew very quiet. Annamarie was aware of only the slow beating of the clock on the shelf, sounding loud in the silent room. It seemed to say: *Brad . . . Brad . . . Brad. . . How can I ever forget* his laughing eyes, his merry grin? she agonized.

When Annamarie awoke the next morning the wind had died, and thin pink sunlight filtered through the clouds, glistening on uneven wads of fog. She hoped the schoolhouse would warm up quickly before the pupils came.

To her surprise Harry Jensen was there when she arrived, stirring the feebly burning embers in the heater and adding more chips.

"Thought I'd come early and build a fire for ya, bein's it's tolerable cold today. Sure will be glad when spring comes," he said, rattling the grate as he nursed the sputtering flame with more chips. He paused and turned to face her. "I wanted to tell you I was sorry to hear that your sweetheart was killed on the Plains. It's as I told ya — them Injun fights is sure chancey."

Annamarie's heart beat faster. She hoped

Harry wouldn't try to con her into renewing his courtship now that he felt Brad was no longer a threat.

"Harry —"

"I know I like you a lot, and you are a purty little thing, and sure need someone bad right now." He rubbed his hands together nervously. "I'm buildin' this nice little house, like I told ya, and we'd have made a good team."

"Harry — please . . ." she faltered lamely.

"But I hope ya don't mind, Annamarie. I — I like your little friend even more. She reminds me of a chirky little brown sparrow. She's so — well, she's clever and sweet and says she won't mind livin' on a farm up here. I wanted you to know — I'd spoke to you first, and if you'd still rather have me since your feller's gone, I'd do the right thing and tell Emmy Lou —"

Relief flooded over Annamarie's face. "Oh, no, Harry. You're so right for her, and she's right for you. The two of you are made for each other. What's happened to Brad was — tragic. But that's neither here nor there now. I'm glad you love my best friend. Just make her happy."

"You give me a chance to show ya!" he burst eagerly, pushing a lock of straw-colored hair. "Long about June my house will be ready and we'll have a nice weddin' with your Pastor Nash tyin' the knot — if she'll have me. You think she will? God will be in our marriage, ya know."

That's how it should be, she thought. *I'm happy for Emmy Lou to have found her life's partner — even if I —* Pain knifed through her heart again. *Oh, dear God, will it always be this way?*

Just then she heard a scuffle of feet as the door burst open and the Culp twins tumbled inside, their coats and scarves the same tangle of blue.

"Oh, Miss Tate! Miss Tate!" Phenie chirped and Phosie echoed, "Yes, Miss Tate."

"We're glad you're back," the words jumbled together.

In the background Roxy's adenoidal twang rang out, "Biss Tate! Biss Tate! We just gotta sig ' 'Tis Sprigtibe, 'tis Sprigtibe, cold widter is past . . .' We're tired of the cold weather!"

The ice in Annamarie's heart had seemed to melt just a little, too.

CHAPTER 17

March came in neither like a lamb nor like a lion, but more like a lumbering, stolid ox, with winds that crooned quietly as they moved across the prairies in slow motion. High woolly clouds hung without movement, their curded bases dipping into the folded valleys beyond the draw. Low, flushed clouds of sunset lingered in the west.

Emmy Lou had blown excitedly into the Tate house one Saturday afternoon when Annamarie returned from her week of teaching. The two girls were upstairs where Annamarie was unpacking her valise in the girls' bedroom.

"Oh, Annamarie," Emmy Lou breathed. "It's really true! Harry wants to marry me . . . and move into his homestead over the hill from Clear Ridge School. Isn't that exciting?"

She bubbled with joy, her speckled face almost beautiful in its plainness as she curled on the bed and watched Annamarie take out the wrinkled clothes from her bag.

"Yes, I know, Emmy Lou," Annamarie

said tossing the crumpled dresses on the bed. "He said he loved you, and that you're as cute as a chirky brown sparrow. I told him what a special person you are, and that he'd better take good care of you. You're more like a wren, you know!"

"I never dreamed I could be so happy . . . except," she paused and got up awkwardly, walking around the room.

"Except what, Emmy Lou?"

"I —" she stammered, her brown face crimson. "I just don't feel right about being so happy when you . . . when Brad."

Annamarie lay down the last wrinkled garment on the bed and came toward her friend. "The Lord has planned our lives from the foundations of the world, and if He had planned for you to marry Harry, that's how it will be. As for me, well, when He maps out our lives, who are we to complain? Somehow, He'll make another way for me to face the future," she added somberly. "I've prayed . . . and all I know is that I must leave it in His care."

The two girls embraced, and Annamarie wiped a tear from her eyes. Life no doubt would take on a new twist. There wasn't much else left to do but accept God's will, was there?

With a sigh she dropped her arms and

tacked a smile onto her face as they sat down on the bed again.

"When my school closes at the end of this month I'll help you get ready for your wedding. I'll even stitch up new sheets and pillow shams and hem dish towels." Her words trailed away. She traced the design on the bedspread with her forefinger. Those were all things she'd hoped to do for her own home some day. Her mother had taken in two more boarders who came only for noon meals, and with the money added to their meager funds, things were looking up for the Tates.

Emmy Lou's bright smile faded. "Thank you, my dear friend. I'm sure I'll finish everything by June. My mother's working on a star quilt now." She paused and sighed. "Most girls here in Council Grove are always hemming dish towels and piecing quilts, but you don't hear of Linda Corling working on things like that."

"Perhaps she's never learned to do any handwork."

"But she hasn't even mentioned quilts and dish towels! Maybe she gave up hope after . . . after she knew Brad really loved you."

Annamarie looked up. "Perhaps, if she does get ready for a wedding, she can afford to buy all her household needs from the big shops in the East."

"Well, she seems to have lost interest in any young men since Brad left. And have you noticed how pale and thin she looks?"

"Yes, for a long time. I . . . I haven't visited her in some weeks," Annamarie said slowly. "But, yes, you're right. She doesn't look at all well. Could the loss of Brad's life have affected her that much?"

"She was always rather queer, I guess. I never really liked her very much. Ever since she came she's kept to herself. I never could see how you even tried to befriend her."

Annamarie toyed with the wrist of her sleeve. "I did it only because Brad asked me to. Maybe I was wrong about her. I thought she was too prissy, too perfect, and I never really became her friend. Somehow I hope she'll bear up under the strain of Brad's . . . death, the same as I'm trying to do. But, Emmy Lou, she doesn't seem to know our Savior! Maybe if she did —"

"Well, I won't have time to make friends with her now. I've got so much work to do! I have a wedding to plan, you know."

"Yes. And this very afternoon I'll help you hem dishtowels and table cloths. Let's tell my mother that I'll devote myself to you, Emmy Lou, on weekends."

The two girls hurried down the stairs, told Mrs. Tate about their intentions and left the house, chattering about wedding plans as they went.

Just as they rounded the corner, Bertha Bennett, Brad's mother met them. She wore a neat tidy gingham dress and pert dark blue jacket. Her hair was deep brown like Brad's, and she wore a shapely toque on her head. Yet her face looked drawn and sad. Instinctively Annamarie reached out a hand in sympathy.

"Oh, Mrs. Bennett," she began, then paused awkwardly.

The woman threw her arms around Annamarie and pressed her close.

"My dear Annie," she said in a low, husky voice, "I'm so, so sorry. Not only for Brad's father and myself, but for you as well. If Brad hadn't met his death by the Indians, you'd have been our daughter! When I see you in church, I can almost hear the two of you singing, 'Oh, for a Closer Walk with God.' I think of how much pain you must have! I wanted to tell you that no matter what's happened, our Bradford loved the Lord. And trying to save Po-a-be's life is exactly what he'd do, without thought of his own safety. Just as he tried to be Linda's strength, her shield. It's the way Brad is . . . was. Perhaps knowing this will make it easier for you."

Annamarie nodded, unable to speak. But what did she mean, Linda's strength? Why had he been at her side so much? Tears stung Annamarie's eyes and she swallowed the lump in her throat.

"I'm trying to understand. But whatever there was between Brad and Linda, I've never heard about it. She hinted once that there was something. Maybe I'll never know."

Mrs. Bennett drew back. "I will insist that she tell you. You've every right to know. Please believe me, I still look upon you as being Brad's. His father and I have made a will and you will receive Brad's share. We want it that way."

"Oh!" A gasp escaped her and she clasped her hand over her mouth. "I . . . It's very kind of you, but you needn't feel —"

"Oh, but that's how we want it. Before Brad left for Ohio to attend college, we looked forward to the time when you two would be married, for he's always told us you were God's choice for him. He said he asked you to wait for him. But then there came the time when he . . . when you . . . had a misunderstanding. I assume it was because of Linda, somehow. Brad was never very good about expressing himself, so he didn't say much. But I knew it affected him very deeply. He felt so strongly about going to fight the Indians because he wanted to make the Plains safe for the settlers. I trust you understand?"

Annamarie nodded again. Tears choked her voice. "Mrs. Bennett, he asked me what he should do — go or stay. I . . . I told him the answer lay between him and God. I'm sure he had found his answer. But I'll regret to my dying day that I didn't tell him good-bye."

The two women looked at each other in silence, then without another word, they embraced. The older woman stepped back and walked away. Annamarie knew she would never forget the tears in Brad's mother's eyes.

Emmy Lou took her arm and the two started silently down the street. Then Annamarie squeezed her friend's arm.

"Oh, why didn't I tell him goodbye? Why was I so stubborn and stupid? May God forgive me!"

"Annamarie, God knows you're sorry. So if you'll just —"

"But that doesn't change things. Brad must've wondered often why I refused to speak to him, yet he kept right on loving me.

If only I had known what was between Brad and Linda, it might have been easier."

Emmy Lou stopped short. "Then you'll have to ask her. Make her tell you!"

"No, I won't force it from her. Maybe it's because I'm afraid to know what it was," she said lamely. "Yet it's good to know Brad's parents had hoped Brad and I —" She started down the street again.

"Well, that's more than Linda has to console her."

"Whatever it is, the Lord knows. All I can do is trust Him one day at a time."

The two girls had reached the Hanks' shabby cottage, and Emmy Lou opened the door.

"We'd better get busy if your dowry's to be ready for June," Annamarie said with a stab at cheerfulness. "As Roxy would say, 'You're a Jude bride, you dow.' " And they both burst out laughing.

I never thought I'd laugh again, Annamarie told herself. But the conversation with Brad's mother had somehow buoyed her spirits. A bit more of the ice around her heart had melted. Maybe some day she could look back without the awful, wrenching pain. Or maybe something would happen so she could forget the past.

CHAPTER 18

It was hard to believe the end of the school year had come, and this was her last day at the Clear Ridge schoolhouse.

The weather had turned mild and windows were left open to allow the soft spring breezes to waft through the room.

The "last day of school" was a community affair, she learned, when the district swarmed to the schoolhouse as mothers brought baskets of fried chicken and boiled eggs, pickled beets from last summer's canning and freshly-baked dried apple pies still warm from the oven. Planks had been laid across the desks and the food piled on the boards. Someone had pumped a large bucket of drinking water with a dipper from the well. Aromas of baked sweet potatoes and stewed apples drifted over the room as mothers set out the food they had brought.

"Wonder if the Kremeiers will bring a potful of cooked cabbage again," Mrs. Field whispered into Annamarie's ear. "What else could they contribute?"

Annamarie smiled. "I think I saw Mrs.

Kremeier come in with a pan of what looked like potatoes and onions."

"Onions! Well, that's a switch. Where'd they get potatoes and onions?"

Mrs. Field began to lift lids to peek and sniff the contents of each kettle. "Probably potatoes took the least effort to fix!" she snorted. "Mrs. Kremeier don't work any-more'n she has to."

The clatter of tin plates and cups echoed through the room as the hungry crowd stood in line to dish up their dinner. Roxy giggled in one corner with her plate heaped high as she tried to catch Walter's eyes. He seemed oblivious to her come-hither look.

One by one the line thinned and the rattle of flatware grew less. A few mothers walked about the classroom and looked over the schoolwork Annamarie had tacked onto the walls, exclaiming over the neat penmanship and arithmetic problems the children had solved.

Suddenly Mrs. Field let out a shriek. "Zack Field, what's the matter with you? Your name ain't Zachary Taylor Field, and you know it! Why can't you stick to the truth? The very idea!"

Annamarie smiled. No doubt Mrs. Field was unwilling to allow her son the dignity of bearing the name of the former president! It might have given him incentive to make something of himself in the future.

Finally the dinner was over, after which school board members John Fromm and Buck Willis dismantled the makeshift tables. Annamarie got the broom from the corner closet and swept up the crumbs and told the children to get ready for the afternoon's entertainment.

It was rather an impromptu agenda of numbers the pupils had prepared. She had given them permission to recite anything they had wished, and now they sat as quietly as possible in the front waiting for the afternoon's program to begin. Annamarie hurried to the rear of the room and peered into the cracked mirror that hung on the wall as she tucked a few stray curls into place, tidied up her hair and straightened the red bow on the front of her blue dress. Already, the parents settled into the seats with a low murmur of voices. The pupils whispered and giggled in anticipation.

She marched to the front of the room and waved for silence. "The children have prepared a short program for you this afternoon," she said. "Most of the numbers are things they learned during the past months. We'll open with Walter Kremeier reading the 23rd Psalm."

Walter swaggered to the front in his

patched trousers, fumbled through his Bible and began to read:

"The Lord is my Shepherd, I shall not want — *anything* . . ."

A few snickers followed his improvised heartfelt wish, after which the Culp twins trotted to the front and sang "Jack and Jill went up the Hill" in a sing-song rhythm. Roxy Field recited "Bistress Bary Quite Codtrary" in her usual twang, and Mae Kremeier quoted "Hot Cross Buns." In the row behind her, Annamarie overheard Mrs. Field whisper rather loudly, "Of course, her poem's about food!" Annamarie amended the thought, "I s'pose they never have enough."

Just when she thought the program was over, Roxy sashayed to the front once more, curtsied and cleared her throat.

"I learned a poem Biss Tate didn't know or didn't think I'd say. But it was so purty I learned it by heart so I'll say it."

And she waded through Henry Wadsworth Longfellow's *Paul Revere's Ride* without a single mistake, ending with the cryptic words, "The bidnight bessage of Paul Revere." All the while Annamarie's neck grew more red with embarrassment at each fresh line of the lengthy poem.

To her surprise the applause was deafening. She struggled to her feet and stood before the beaming audience after the clapping ended and said, "That was quite an accomplishment, Roxy! Of course, as you can see, Clear Ridge pupils worked hard, and I'm very proud of them. This concludes our afternoon's program. I wish each one of you a good summer. Thanks, all of you, for coming."

After the entertainment, one parent after another made their way to her side.

"That was a fine program, Miss Tate. One of the best we've ever had!"

"You'll be back with us next fall, won't you?"

"You were such a good teacher."

The words were different, of course, but the sentiment from each one was the same. All she could say was to mumble a weak, "I've enjoyed teaching here very much, but I haven't quite decided."

"You ain't gettin' married, are you? We'd hoped you'd marry Harry and settle right amongst us," Buck Willis said bluntly.

Lizzie Powers sidled toward her. "Now, now, Annamarie," she clucked, "you gotta come back. Me and Ben liked havin' you stayin' with us!"

Annamarie drew a deep breath. *Dear Lord,* she prayed silently, *what will You have me to do? I haven't found the answer yet. Please let me know soon.*

CHAPTER 19

The April afternoon had turned warm and humid as the early spring heat shimmered and dipped in the scant shade of the elms. Then the late afternoon air grew stagnant.

Annamarie lay on the sofa and fanned herself with the latest issue of the *Advertiser*, batting the warm air around her hot face.

Her school was over for the year and she had packed her school materials away into cardboard boxes and pushed them to the far end of the cupboard. She still hadn't given Clear Ridge the answer they had asked for. Although she had enjoyed her school term she hadn't agreed to come back in the fall, and she couldn't understand why.

Time had grown boring, and even Emmy Lou had become too busy for frequent visits. Besides, Emmy Lou hadn't protested much when her friend didn't want to become very involved with her wedding plans. Perhaps she understood how it reminded Annamarie of Brad.

Annamarie tried to excuse herself, "Mother needs me to help with the garden and the house." She argued with her conscience, "And I must lend Susan a hand with her schoolwork since the school in town isn't over."

The spring and summer loomed ahead gloomy and gray. Without Emmy Lou, how would she spend her days? The Dillon girls and the Hammond sisters had never made strong efforts to become close friends. It seemed that boarding house work was all she had to look forward to.

With a sigh she got up and began to pace back and forth. Mentally she debated about paying a visit to Linda Corling, but frankly, she didn't want to. What could she say to the moody girl without offending her?

Just then she heard the whinny of a horse on the street and she walked to the window. Who was at the hitching post in front of the house? Laying down her fan she hurried to the door. A thin, stooped figure dropped from the back of the Corlings' fine black stallion and walked to the porch.

Stepping out on the porch she shaded her eyes against the glare of the sun with her hand.

"Linda? Is there something I can do for you?"

Linda raised her stricken eyes. "Annamarie, I must . . . I must talk to you! Will you please ride out to the draw with me?"

"To the draw? But why so far when it's so muggy?"

"Maybe we can sit in the cool shade of the cottonwood. I must tell you something I should've told you a long time ago. Please come with me now!"

Pausing only a moment to call to Susan that she was riding out with Linda Corling, Annamarie snatched her bonnet and hurried into the barn and threw the saddle on Lady's back. Then swinging herself astride she nudged the horse toward the end of the street and turned to the open meadow. Linda followed meekly. The prairies were beautiful at any hour of the day, but Annamarie loved them especially in the springtime when they rippled and blended into unbroken tapestries studded with wildflowers.

The girls rode silently down the steep slope that stretched indefinitely toward the draw. Annamarie wondered if Linda was at last ready to reveal her secret. The thin white face was taut and drawn, showing a hint of what this puzzling thing was about.

After riding down the faint path, they turned their horses toward the big cottonwood that spread its broad branches over the right side of the draw. Here, the watershed between the Neosho River was only a high swell, and straight toward the west it became level as a floor.

Linda drew up her horse toward the tree and slid from its sweaty back while Annamarie paused to tie Lady's reins loosely on the lower branches of the tree. When she looked up, Linda had thrown herself in the shade and pillowed her head on the back of her arms. Annamarie lowered herself to the ground and lay down beside her, her arms behind her head.

"Well, here we are, Linda," she said lightly. "It's beastly warm for this time of year, and it might have been cooler at home with glasses of lemonade on the shady north porch."

Linda shook her head. "No. I wanted us to be alone, Annamarie. Here . . . here's where Brad and I rode once when he wanted to show me this big tree, but —"

"But what?"

"The tree is so large, so shady, that I felt dwarfed by its size."

"Yes, it is a big tree. Brad and I have ridden out here many times in the summer twilight to bring home the cows for milking. I don't know how often we paused to linger and watch the sunset —"

"Please don't, Annamarie!" Linda cut in sharply. "That's not what I want to talk about."

Annamarie drew a deep breath. "Then what is it you want to tell me?"

A long, sigh escaped the pale, thin girl. "It all began when I met Brad Bennett at the college in Ohio. I knew right away he was very, very special. But he lost no time in telling me that, although he would always be my friend, he had a girl waiting for him back in Kansas. I knew it from the beginning, but I was so sure." She paused again.

"So sure of what, Linda?"

"That . . . just maybe I'd get well enough so he'd fall in love with me, especially when my father offered him all that money to set him up in business for himself. He would've been a very wealthy businessman. He could've had anything he wanted."

"But you said, 'to be well enough.' What did that mean?"

Tears formed in the green eyes and cut shiny paths down the wan cheeks.

"That's the secret, Annamarie. I have . . . I have a rare, incurable blood disease, one that will eventually claim my life. When we first came here to live, the fresh, strong prairie air was therapeutic and I actually grew better. I began to hope I'd get fully well."

A rare blood disease? A feeling of pity surged through Annamarie. She wasn't sure she understood.

"I made Brad promise not to tell a soul! He was so fine and gallant, and I thought that maybe I could get well after all, so he'd want to marry me. He'd have anything he wanted." She turned to look into Annamarie's eyes, "I schemed and planned and I even stole the letter you left for him and those he wrote to you in the Hermit's Cave! But when I opened his and read them —"

"You read Brad's letters to me, Linda? But why?" Her words were harsh.

"Because I wanted to know if he cared for you as much as he said he did. I found out he meant every word. And no amount of money would betray his love for you."

"But why didn't you tell me you were ill? I might have understood —"

Linda shook her blond head fiercely. "I didn't want your pity! But as time went by I realized I was growing weaker. Then Brad went away to fight the Cheyennes and I knew I'd lost him for good. I knew I had to tell you as he'd begged me to, but as long as I felt I stood a chance, I held off. I blamed you for his death!

"The last checkup I had with Dr. Mason in St. Louis I realized how sick I was and I gave up. The doctor says there's no hope. Annamarie, I know I'm dying, and I — oh," she sobbed. "I'm so terribly afraid to die! If

I die tomorrow I know I wouldn't be ready to meet God! You've always seemed so confident, so strong and have so much faith. So I knew it was time I told you everything! I've been awful to you and I'm so sorry. Oh, Annamarie, can you forgive me? Will the Lord forgive me?"

The hot air of the afternoon had grown very still and stagnant, and the birds had ceased their aimless twittering.

Annamarie knelt at Linda's side and touched the thin shoulders. She spoke in a low voice. "The Bible says that 'all have sinned, and come short of the glory of God,' and for as many as received him, to them He gives the power to become the sons of God, and those who come to Him He will not cast out. You've heard Pastor Nash preach this, haven't you?"

Linda sat up, her green eyes filled with tears. "Yes, but I didn't know he was talking about me! How could I ever accept all that love and forgiveness and grace after what I've done to you?"

"It means everyone. God is so merciful. No matter how good or how bad we've been —"

"Oh, I've been stupid and arrogant!" Linda burst out. "I know that now. If only I had peace in my heart so I wouldn't be afraid." She paused and stared at the sky. "Annamarie, I don't like the looks of those strange clouds in the west! What's going to happen?" She burst out, her voice full of fear.

The ugly black swirling clouds in the west had suddenly covered the horizon as swift, moving darkness cut through the draw.

For a moment Annamarie froze. Then she grabbed Linda's arm and jerked her to her feet. The clouds had grown greenish-gray and had whipped themselves into a bowl in the southeast, a goblet that grew twisted and black and distorted.

Tornado! The word slammed into her head. She knew these funnel-shaped storms sometimes swept swiftly across the Midwest after a warm humid day, and could wreck havoc in seconds. It was too late to ride to safety. Already the horses were stomping and whinnying in frenzy. She untied them quickly, watching as they raced away from the impending storm toward town.

Grabbing Linda she hurried toward the deepest depression she could see on the draw and pushed her down into it, and threw herself in beside her.

"Lie down!" she hissed in her ear, "and keep your face in that shallow depression!" she ordered hoarsely. "Lie perfectly still!"

The two girls lay quietly, cowering in silence. Annamarie felt Linda begin to shake with terror as the wild wind shrieked and whirled angrily toward them . . .

CHAPTER 20

Annamarie threw her arm over Linda's shoulders and whispered into her dainty pink ear:

The LORD is my Shepherd, I shall not want. He maketh me to lie down in green pastures. (Psalms 23:1)

She gulped. "Linda, the Lord *is* our Shepherd, and He cares for us! Do you believe that He loves you — unconditionally?"

Linda whimpered a little, then said something softly that Annamarie couldn't hear. But Linda's voice continued with the psalm in response,

Yea, though I walk through the valley of the shadow of death, I will fear no evil: for thou art with me . . . (23:4)

Annamarie turned her head and looked at the sky. To the southwest the bowl had twisted, blackened and tipped northward as though all the powers of darkness were invited to drink from it. Like the stem of a wine goblet, the narrow tip of the funnel touched the far horizon, poised there for a moment, then swayed dizzily as it moved toward the open county. With a terrible roar it charged over the prairie, sweeping everything in its maw while the earth seemed to bow in frightened silence. Once the stem stretched away from the bowl then resumed its shape again. It moved swiftly, restlessly, erratically. Gracefully it rose up out of a farmer's field, bending and swaying as it came. Then it moved wildly, crazily, toward the ditch where the two girls huddled.

The stem was bending now as if the bowl had become too heavy for it. Upper wind currents began to distort its shape further. Fear began to grip Annamarie as the scene began to look as though the demons had drunk their fill, bent the stem and twisted it in their wrath. To her ears, it sounded like they laughed hilariously as they flung the goblet toward the ditch while the girls cowered in fear.

Annamarie tried to scream but no sound came from her mouth. It felt like cotton and she could hardly swallow. Then the bowl broke slowly and disintegrated over the bare fields. To her surprise the tornado was over.

The whole world lay hushed in the wake

of the relentless fury. Annamarie clenched her hands and tried to speak words that wouldn't come. She was afraid to look at Linda, fearful of what she would read in her stricken green eyes.

Finally she turned her head. Linda sat up with her face calm and serene. A faint smile tugged at her lips.

"Linda?"

"I'm all right, Annamarie. For the first time in my life I'm not afraid. Oh, it's as if God stepped right out of the terrible cloud and held me close. And it was wonderful!"

"I'm so glad for that. It was such an awful ordeal," she gulped out. "Linda, did I hear you say 'yes' when I asked you if you believed that God loved you unconditionally?"

Linda nodded with a smile. She wrapped her arms around herself as a chill went up her spine.

Annamarie smiled back. "We've got to get back to town. You're shivering."

"I wonder if the town is still standing," Linda mused, peering through the murky atmosphere toward the northeast. "But I'm sure it must be. Council Grove seems indestructible, don't you think?"

Annamarie nodded. "I don't think the tornado reached the town. But we'll have to hurry home before it rains."

"Yes. It's only that . . . I'm so very tired."

The dark clouds had moved away swiftly and the sky was deep blue to the east while rain clouds hung in the west. Rain was definitely on the way.

For a few moments all the land was bathed in sunlight and the praire looked yellow-green darkening to verdure along the horizon. Suddenly the clouds piled higher and higher until they hid the late afternoon sun, and the world turned cool and gray. The sweet, deep aroma of the rain swept across the prairie, then down the fields sped a brief summer shower. Annamarie and Linda clung together in the silvery mist, their clothes soaking wet in seconds as they pressed on down the path.

Mud oozed around their feet as they moved up the blurred, rocky trail. Linda looked so weary that Annamarie almost despaired of helping her to town as she tried to bear much of Linda's weight on her right shoulder. Now and then they sat down on a large rock to rest, for Linda was very weak, and Annamarie had to be her support as they struggled forward.

Yet the girl seemed so serene and quiet as she said, "God saves us from our sins and from tornados. Will you forgive me, too, Annamarie?"

Now Annamarie was sure that Linda had encountered the Holy Spirit in that ditch in the draw. She answered without hesitation, "Yes, Linda."

The birds had taken up their singing again, and the fields glistened from the raindrops. Apparently the tornado had skipped past the town, and all that remained of the havoc was an occasional flattened fence post.

The sun was lowering in the west when Annamarie half-carried, half-dragged Linda to the porch of the pretentious Corling home. The maid let them in and scurried Linda off to the bedroom.

Annamarie could barely speak. It was as though all her energy had been poured into Linda to bring her back.

Mrs. Corling pattered anxiously into the room, her upswept coiffure straggling with hairpins.

"Oh, you're back! I was so worried when we noticed the dark clouds in the west. Then Prince came trotting home without Linda. I had begged her not to go but she was so stubborn and wouldn't listen. It was 'something she had to do,' she said." She stared curiously at Annamarie who had seated herself hesitantly on the edge of a chair, for her legs ached. "I s'pose she's told you everything?" she added.

"Yes." Annamarie nodded. "She told me. But in spite of the awful storm one blessed thing happened."

Mrs. Corling's face became a startled frown. "What in the world could have happened that was good? She could have died, you know." She stared at the mud-stained ruffle on Annamarie's dress.

"Mrs. Corling, Linda finally made Jesus Christ her Savior! Now she won't have to live in fear any more."

A strange look swept over Mrs. Corling's face. "I'm not sure I understand what you mean. Linda has never had to be afraid of anything! We've surrounded her with everything good, everything possible. Well, thank you for bringing her home. Now I must go to her room. You can let yourself out."

Without a backward look Annamarie left the house, making her way wearily down the street.

I think I've finally begun to understand Linda Corling, she told herself as she walked down the gravel path. No, the Corlings have not given their daughter everything. God had not been part of her life until now. *I think I might've really been her friend, if I'd known sooner.*

She now realized that Brad was only being kind to Linda and would never have considered marrying the girl, even though her father had offered to set him up in business. But why Linda hadn't wanted anyone to know she was ill was a mystery. Perhaps it was because she'd thought she was getting better. The fresh, brisk Kansas air had invigorated her and she had hoped she would recover after all. Yet Annamarie knew deep in her heart that Brad would never marry someone who wasn't committed to Jesus Christ. Well, out there in the draw Linda had made that commitment. It was too bad Brad would never know.

Once on Pine Street, she looked for Lady, who waited patiently at the stable door with the mud-splattered saddle slightly tilted on her back. After removing the saddle and stabling the horse, she went indoors. She plopped into a chair and proceeded to tell her mother and Susan of the traumatic tornado event and of the situation with Linda.

"But through it all, God was good. Linda surrendered to Him. I trust she'll rest up for a few days. She was so very tired. She is really terribly ill."

CHAPTER 21

The next morning when Graham Scott answered the sharp knock at the door, it was Mary, the Corlings' maid. She looked very distraught.

"It's Miss Linda," she sobbed aloud. "She up and died last night! I'm on my way into town, so I thought I'd stop by to tell you about it."

Linda — dead! Annamarie gasped at the abrupt message and stifled a sob.

Had I only known, I might have been a better friend these past months. The girl had always been pale and fragile, but I figured it was her nature, she thought.

"Oh, Graham, it must have all been too much for her — the tornado, the soaking rain, the unburdening of her heart." She called to the maid, who was turning to go. "Thank you for letting us know, Mary."

Graham nodded, "Our condolences to the Corling family."

It seemed incredible that Linda was gone. *I should've suspected she was ill before this,* Annamarie chided herself after she had visited the Corling home where the wake was held. *I thank God for His faithfulness to her. I never kept my promise to Brad to be her friend. Perhaps, had I known, I would have acted differently.*

Annamarie, back in her room after the burial service, decided to face a few facts herself. Not only had she reneged in her relationship with Brad when she had been sure he had been unfaithful in his promise to her, but she also had refused to tell him goodbye when the boys left to join the Kansas cavalry.

"Lord, please forgive me!" she cried as she lay on the bed with her tears and regrets. "It's too late now for Brad and me. But I could've been a better friend to Linda, maybe encouraged her as a friend or told her about You."

She blew her nose and sat up in bed.

Now she had to pick up the pieces of her shattered life and go on. She still hadn't decided about going back to Clear Ridge for the fall term. She loved her pupils devotedly in spite of their quirks and it made her life more interesting. Why couldn't she make up her mind to go back?

She smoothed her rumpled pink gingham, combed her mussed brown hair and went downstairs. Her mother was already preparing the evening meal, bending over the panful of potatoes she was peeling for frying. The garden had yielded its first crop of peas.

"It's time to put them on to cook," Mrs. Tate said. "Susan's unhappy about picking those early ones. She says they're too scrawny. But boiled with our onions and a spot of butter, they're quite tasty. I've noticed how much Graham likes them."

"Does he? Well, he seems to like anything you cook, Mother," Annamarie said, tying her blue apron around her waist as she tackled the biscuit making.

"Yes, he's an honorable young man." Her mother looked up from her work. "Brad departed to his eternal reward months ago. Have you been aware how much Graham likes you?"

Annamarie's blue eyes widened and she wiped her floury hands on her apron.

"Mother! Why, he . . . he knows how much I loved Brad. Surely he can't think I'm ready to fall in love with anyone else ever again!"

"Why not? He's hinted to me more than once that he'd be mightily pleased if you'd marry him. He's a faithful Christian, and he'd be very good to you."

"Mother! But I loved Brad and I always shall. Surely you don't expect . . . I don't think I can ever love again. That's the way it is."

Her mother sliced the boiled potatoes into a skillet on the stove. "Better hurry those biscuits into the oven. The boarders will be home in less than half an hour."

Silently Annamarie finished stirring up the saleratus biscuits and shaped them deftly with an overturned cup. Graham Scott! The idea was ridiculous. How in the world could she ever consider marrying anyone but Brad! Anyone who thought this had to be stupid.

As she set the panful of biscuits in the oven she turned to her mother. "Clear Ridge has begged me to come back for the fall term. I haven't given them an answer, but it surely isn't because I have plans to marry again, as they seem to think!"

She picked up the pile of plates from the cupboard and set the table. The aroma of frying potatoes and bubbling peas on the range filled the kitchen. Her face was red and flushed as thoughts pummeled in her head. *I don't love Graham. Yes, he's been a good friend, but I didn't think he had marriage on his mind!*

What should she do? This was incredible. She never, never would have dreamed . . .

At that moment the outside door opened

and Graham and Editor Johnson came in for supper. At the wash basin, they washed up as she sliced the wheat bread and set a jar of blackberry jam on the table. A freshly-baked gingerbread sent aromas of spice as she cut it into generous squares. She kept her face turned away from them and worked to complete supper preparations.

Susan had come in from feeding the chickens with a basket of fresh eggs, sniffing the heady fragrance of supper.

When there was nothing left to do, Annamarie took her place at the table and sat down, looking at the plate. *I don't want to face him,* she thought. *He isn't Brad Bennett! There's no way.*

"Will you return thanks, Graham?" she heard her mother say.

"With pleasure," Graham said, his rich voice intoning the words addressed to the Heavenly Father. "Our blessed Lord, be Thou our guide and bless this food Thou hast provided for us, to Thy honor and glory." Somehow the words were more meaningful than she had ever realized. Yes, the Lord had provided for their sustenance. She would have to trust Him to continue to lead.

Amid the table chatter, Annamarie remained quiet — until Johnson turned to her.

"I saw Roxy and her brother in town today. They were with their mother to subscribe to the *Advertiser*. Nice, well-behaved children."

Annamarie looked up. "Yes, that they are. Except one might find Roxy's adenoids a bit irritating after a while," she said. "One day one of the children mentioned that in the big cities people were saying, 'Breakfast, lunch and dinner,' instead of 'breakfast, dinner and supper.' Roxy and her brother found it quite amusing."

"Yes, I'm sure some folks are convinced that it's written in stone as breakfast, dinner and supper!" Graham quipped.

Laughter erupted around the table at the joke. Annamarie hadn't wanted to appear aloof but she didn't join in their laughter.

"Annamarie, you're so quiet I wondered what was wrong. Of course, I know you've lost your friend, Linda, a few days ago, but I heard you were the person who showed her to the Savior. Maybe you should consider being a missionary."

"Oh, no . . ." she replied. "I'd never fit the part! I wouldn't want to live in some foreign land." She paused awkwardly. "I mean —"

"But the Lord could use you in His service right here in our country! There are many Indians who have not yet heard the gospel."

She was driven into silence again. Never had she felt the call to spread the gospel in the manner that she supposed Graham had intended and much less to the Indians.

After supper, she and Susan washed the dishes and she helped their mother put the food away.

The late April evening had grown cool, and Annamarie decided to take a stroll outdoors. The yellow prairie moon had tip-toed into the evening sky. She turned to her mother. "It's a beautiful evening. I want to take a walk, for I have this urge to be alone."

"Of course. Be sure to take a wrap. It's still cool this time of year."

She picked up her light jacket and let herself out the door. She walked up the cliff path which lay bright and clear in the moonlight like a shiny yellow ribbon. Stars began to wink in the evening sky.

I wonder if I'll ever be able to forget Brad and the many times we walked up this path together, she thought.

Suddenly she heard footsteps behind her, and a stab of pain shot through her. Brad? Of course not!

"Hello, Annamarie!" Graham's voice called out cheerfully. "I thought you might like someone to walk with you on this gorgeous evening. May I?"

She paused awkwardly. "I — I suppose it wouldn't hurt."

"Wouldn't hurt!" he laughed boyishly. "It would give me a great deal of pleasure." He took her arm, and together they made their way up the moonlit road. She stiffened, and for a moment she almost imagined it was Brad beside her.

They walked silently until they reached the big flat boulder which provided a place to stop and rest.

"Let's sit here for a few minutes," Graham said, seating her graciously on the rock, then stood beside her. "This place is beautiful in the moonlight, isn't it?"

Annamarie caught her breath sharply. "Brad and I . . . we walked here often. There are so many memories."

"I don't mean to barge in on your memories, but . . . you know, I've grown to love you, Annamarie. I wonder if, now that Brad is gone, you would do me the honor of marrying me?" His words came out in a rush.

"Marry you!" she gasped. "Graham Scott, Brad's only been gone for about five months!"

"Maybe you need more time, but I really want to marry you, my dear."

She shook her head. "Graham, you're a minister of the gospel. What would I know about helping you in your work?" she flared, not knowing what else to say.

"Just exactly what you did for Linda Corling during her last hours. You're sensitive, kind and devoted to our Lord. Please think about it. You see, I've been asked to take a church near Emporia. They don't want a single pastor. I know I'm not a dashing romantic, but I do love you. I promise to make you happy."

"Knowing I don't love you, Graham?"

"Brad can't come back! I'll do my best to make you forget him, although I cannot promise that you will ever fully do that."

Annamarie was silent. She had considered the idea as being ridiculous, but she knew Graham was right. Brad would never come back. Graham was kind, conscientious and considerate. He had a wry sense of humor and to be his wife would give her other things to think about.

Was this the reason the Lord hadn't given her peace about going back to Clear Ridge to teach? Maybe it was time to make an effort to put Brad and the past out of her mind. She knew it was a decision not to be made lightly. Her mother was doing well with her boarding house, and with Emmy Lou to be married in June, it would mean a chance to look forward to a new life.

"Graham," she began awkwardly, "I just don't know —"

"Say yes, Annamarie," he said with a pleading look that furrowed his eyebrows in earnest. "I need to be married no later than early summer, for that's when my ministry's to begin. I promise you won't be sorry."

She stared at the moon shining in the sky. In the bushes she heard crickets chirping. It was a peaceful scene. In the deepening prairie twilight that night, she finally faced the fact that Brad would never come back.

She spoke softly in reply, "I suppose I could, if you want me to." She could tell by Graham's face that her words pleased him very much.

In the days that followed, Annamarie moved in a world wholly apart from the past. The door to a home of her own through which she had looked so often was wide open now. All she dreamed and longed for as Mrs. Bennett, the banker's wife, was to come true for her as Mrs. Scott, the minister's wife.

May dragged by. Now Annamarie lived only in a world of preparation, a very commonplace world in which one hemmed sheets and pieced quilts for a strange man who said he wanted to marry her.

One Sunday Graham decided they would drive out early in his buggy to the small white country church near Emporia which he was to pastor. Annamarie looked pretty in a new pale blue cape her mother had made for her. It was very full and came to the bottom of her dress, the collar trimmed with a bit of lace. The church was filled when they arrived and the congregation greeted them warmly. There was a dinner afterwards to which everyone came, although Annamarie ate without appetite.

"We'll clean that small house over there and fix it up as a parsonage. We'll put up new curtains and provide rugs," the women told her.

Yet the prospect didn't excite Annamarie in the least. It was like a storybook happening, unreal and inconceivable. But she had promised Graham so she'd go through with it, no matter what.

It was late afternoon when they got into the buggy and rode back to Council Grove. She was very quiet most of the way. Now Graham turned to her.

"Annamarie, I hope you're happy about your promise to marry me. I know you loved Brad, but please remember I love you very much. I'll do all I can to make you happy."

She nodded faintly. "I know, Graham. Yet it doesn't seem right somehow to marry someone I don't love."

"By God's grace we'll serve Him together. The people in that little church loved you, you know. The women have all sorts of plans to fix up the parsonage. Please be happy!" His big hand stole over her small one lying in her lap.

Tears filled her eyes as the buggy rolled into town in the early dusk. Already the sun had set behind the rim of low hills as shreds of cloud caught fire in the flame and tumult of a windy sunset that spread over half the sky.

She stared into the oncoming darkness in silence. All through the night she thought about Brad, about Graham, about everything that had happened in the past and would possibly happen in the future, and the tears came to her eyes again.

"But nothing can make a difference now," she mumbled to herself in the blackness. "I promised Graham, and I won't go back on my promise."

Emmy Lou had been delighted when she had heard of Annamarie's plans to marry Graham, and the two girls discussed wedding plans on the Tates' porch as they sat on the swing that Graham had made.

"Don't tell me you'll get ahead of me and move away!" Emmy Lou protested playfully. "You promised to stand up with Harry and me, and now you'll marry Graham the first week in June, a week before our wedding!"

"It's only because he's promised to take over that church, and that time is rushing up fast."

"Yes, and I'm very happy for you. That you've decided to give up grieving for Brad and make a new life for yourself."

Annamarie sighed. "I suppose you could say that. Grieving won't help and I can help him with his work in the church."

She thought, *Emmy Lou looks so alive, so excited about getting married. But I'm merely existing. Maybe all the frozen ice around my heart will melt someday. Dear Lord, I pray that it will.*

She finally wrote to John Fromm that she wouldn't be back to teach at Clear Ridge. Yes, she was being married in June, as they'd suspected. "I loved all the children," she added. "They helped enrich my life, and I'm thankful for the privilege and the part I had in being their teacher."

The days of May rushed along too fast, and Annamarie decided to walk out to the Hermit's Cave one more time. Soon she'd leave Council Grove and she must put all the many memories behind her forever.

As she made her way cautiously up the path one afternoon, she heard footsteps behind her, and looked up to see who it was.

"Po-a-be!" she cried as her young Indian friend pattered toward her on moccasinned feet. "You're alive! Running Elk found you?"

Her dark eyes glowed as she stopped in front of Annamarie and embraced her warmly. "Yes! Graham told me I could find you here. I had to come and tell you. Running Elk came to the Washita and hunted 'til he found me. It took many moons but he would not give up."

She paused and a troubled look crept into her eyes. "Graham tells me you will marry him in a few days. But," she stopped and lowered her eyes, "I have to tell you. Brad Bennett . . . is not dead. He is alive!"

CHAPTER 22

"Brad? Alive? Po-a-be!" Annamarie gasped, reeling toward the Indian girl who steadied her.

"Yes, my friend. It is true. Brad, he save my life. Then the Cheyennes shot him. He fell . . . like he was dead. I thought he was dead. I hid in the deep cracks in the cave, and the Indians did not find me so they went away. Brad lay on the ground long time . . . so much blood. I waited until I was sure they had gone away, then I look again. I see him move a very little bit."

Annamarie sank to the ground and covered her face with her hands. Was this true? *I don't know if I can believe her,* she thought. Jeremy and Ed saw him fall covered with blood. They were so sure he was killed. *But it couldn't be true,* she thought. *He hadn't survived from what Ed said.*

"Po-a-be, please tell me all you know, or how you know. I . . . I just don't know what to believe."

Po-a-be took Annamarie's arm and led her gently down the path toward the Tate's porch. They sat on the steps together.

"I will tell you. Ed and Jeremy and Brad were with the soldiers who came to look for some Cheyennes hiding in the rocks along the Washita. They did not know I was there. When cavalry troop find Cheyennes, I saw chance to try to get away. Brad pointed his gun at the Cheyennes when I ran but he did not kill anyone. They find him and shoot him. I got away and crawled into deep crack in the rocks. I was very still. All was very still. After a long time they looked for me but I was very still. I hid for a long time. Then Cheyennes did not find me and went away."

"But if this is true, where is Brad now?" Annamarie demanded.

"He is in army hospital. He come soon when he is better. They bring him back. You wait for Brad, not marry Graham?"

Annamarie sighed deeply. What was she to do? She had promised Graham and told him she would keep her promise.

"Po-a-be, don't ask me that! I have to think about this."

Stiffly her Indian friend got up and left with a hurt backward look toward Annamarie who continued to sit on the steps and stare off at the distant horizon.

How could she pick out facts when they

were so intertwined with emotions and duty? Where did events leave off and feelings begin? She had cared for Brad from the first day she had known him. She could almost trace the way that her love for him had crept up on her. Their first youthful admiration had grown into something steadier. That unspoken love had called for an answering love from him. It was as though a magic door had opened and she had caught a glimpse of what love could be and the meaning of life.

Then Death closed the door, or so she had thought, and it didn't seem to matter what turn her life took. Was Brad alive and coming home? Ed had been very sure that no one would ever see Brad again.

I must face it, she thought. But what could be done now? Nothing! She had given Graham her word that she would marry him. She was going to be Graham's wife. Why? It seemed appalling now, but it hadn't that evening on the cliff path. "Would you do me the honor of marrying me?" Graham had asked honorably enough. And she had said, "I suppose I could, if you want me to." It was as good as a "yes" to Graham.

But she was so emotionally frozen then like the icy water in the draw in winter. She did what she thought was the right thing, the practical thing, to do. She hadn't meant it to be hypocritical, saying something she did not mean. It was just that because Brad was never to be hers, nothing else mattered. If no one had asked her to marry, that would have been all right too. She might have gone on teaching school.

But every girl had a right to have a home. She had planned to keep Graham's house and make him a good, sensible wife. Yet nothing could keep her from carrying Brad's image in her heart all her life.

The week that followed was a strange one to Annamarie. Her world was like a cardboard stage with puppets like she had seen at the Teacher's Institute in Emporia. And she was the central puppet being pulled into her place by the people helping to prepare for her wedding. A dazed feeling that nothing mattered had clouded her mind. She had prayed for God's direction but He had been silent.

Now it was the day before her wedding to Graham Scott. Brad hadn't returned. Perhaps Po-a-be had been wrong after all. How could she be sure? And Graham did need her help in his church. What other answer was there?

Annamarie tried on the dress her mother

had altered for her. It had come in a box from Uncle Tom. It was an elaborate dress with a tarlatan overskirt. Her mother knelt for a moment to pull at the skirt, then sat back to get a better view. Annamarie stood with her arms out over the flaring gown so she might not crush the white silk trimming on the folds. The long sleeves dropped downwards, displaying the dainty under-sleeves.

Suddenly her mother burst out, "Oh, Annamarie, smile! Smile like a bride. I can't stand it any longer. Are you happy? Is this what you want?"

Annamarie was crying now, shaking with violent sobs, clutching the white frothiness of the skirt. Her mother stood up and put her arm around her shaking shoulders. Finally, after her tears had spent themselves, she wiped her eyes with a lace-edged hand-kerchief her mother handed her.

"No, it's not as I wanted it, but no one shall ever know except you, Mother! Don't worry. I'll be all right," she nodded. "When we're small we think life is simple, but we find that isn't true. There are all sorts of things that happen to change the course of life. No matter what happens, one must do the right thing. Sometimes it's hard to tell what is the right thing. But the Bible says,

'Trust in the Lord with all thine heart; and lean not unto thine own understanding. In all thy ways acknowledge him, and he shall direct thy paths.' Well, the Lord *will* direct my path. I must believe this, as you've taught Susan and me to believe."

She began to fumble with the gown and gently pulled it over her head. Her mother hung up the dress and smiled faintly. "You are so brave, Annamarie, and I'm very proud of you."

"I know I should've stayed to teach at Clear Ridge to help out. You could've used the extra money."

"I didn't tell you, Annamarie, but I finally got word from your Uncle Tom and learned what your father's mission to Topeka was. It seems he had gone there to seek a position for Uncle Tom at the state capital. Well, it all worked out. When Tom arrived, he wrote to me. He's arranged for some funds to be transferred to me, and I'll have a small pension for as long as I live since your father had served in the war. I won't be rich but we'll manage."

"That's wonderful! I'm so happy for you. You always insisted we trust the Lord for our needs and He has provided.

"Now I must go out to the draw, Mother, and find some prairie lilies for my wedding bouquet." She picked up a basket and set out toward the draw. The prairies shimmered and gleamed with color in the late afternoon. The distant hills were outlined by shadowy lines in their deep folds. A rosy light tinted the western sky. Birds twittered in the still air and hovered in the quietness around the broad cottonwood. A patch of blue shone above the branches that seemed to be reaching out to embrace the sky.

She saw the slopes were starred with white daisies and gaudy red prairie lilies. As she picked one bloom after another, she tried to push aside the memories of the time she and Brad had sauntered along this way that evening when he had kissed her the first time. It was something she must forever file away in her memory.

Suddenly she heard the words to their song being sung somewhere in the distance.

Oh for a closer walk with God, a calm and heavenly frame.

She dropped her basket of flowers. She knew it was Brad's voice! She'd recognize his rich bass anywhere. After a few moments she joined in with her soft, vibrant soprano.

*Where is the blessedness I knew, when first
I saw the Lord?*

She was enraptured by the memory of those special Wednesday evenings when she and Brad stood before the congregation at the Brown Jug sharing one hymn book.

Brad's voice rang on,

So shall my walk be close to God, calm and serene my frame.

The rich, resonant words rang out clear and strong through the dusk, and Annamarie drank in the song of the prairie. It melted the ice that had gripped her emotions these past months.

Then she saw Brad coming slowly up the path toward the draw. He paused as he ended the song alone,

So purer light shall make the road that leads me to the Lamb!

When he finished the song, the calm serenity of the draw closed in around them. Not a bird sang. There was no moan of the prairie wind. Nothing but silence.

"Brad! Why are you here?" she whispered hopefully.

"Annie, I came for you. Your mother said I'd find you here."

"Oh, Brad, it's true! I'm so thankful you're still alive."

She watched his face in wonder. Was this really Brad Bennett — injured so horribly on the Plains, believed to be dead — now holding her hand?

"But, Brad," she said abruptly and looked into his smiling eyes.

"But what, Annie?"

Brad's arms where around her now, his lips sweet on hers.

"I love you so, Annie."

"And I love you."

Then remembering tomorrow was her wedding day to Graham Scott, she drew away. "But it's too late."

"There hasn't been a ceremony yet, has there?" Brad looked uncertain.

"No," she whispered.

"Then it isn't too late." He drew back his head and laughed boyishly. "Of course it isn't too late!"

"Oh, Brad, it's a terrible thing . . . such a terrible thing. I promised to marry Graham . . . and I'm scared about breaking that promise!"

"I'll take full responsibility. We love each other. Tell him! Isn't that enough?"

She nodded feebly.

He assured her, "God understands! We'll both go. There won't be any marriage unless it's the Lord and you and *me*."

"Just us . . . and the Lord."

"Nothing can come between us ever again!"

"Nothing . . . anymore." Her voice was low, and she paused as she heard the song of a bird in the branches above. She stroked his tousled hair, and he kissed her again.

"Brad, did you know Linda is dead?"

He nodded and pushed back a few strands of hair from her forehead. "I also heard that you showed her to the Lord. Your mother told me."

"It was during a tornado. I think she died happy that night."

"I'm sure she did," he said, kissing her again. "Oh, Annie, how I missed you! Your face was always in front of me, but I thought I'd never see you again. Thank God, He brought us back together. The verse in Proverbs three tells us to trust in the Lord with all our hearts. Out there on the Plains I tried to follow Him, and He kept me all the way!"

"Yes, but now to tell Graham." She paused awkwardly.

"You're not afraid to face him with me, are you?

"No, not with you."

"Remember, it's you and me forever."

She reminded herself, *"In all thy ways acknowledge Him." How often I have failed the Lord! But I believe this is what He wants for Brad and me, to be together forever. And our song, "Oh for a Closer Walk with God," that is forever, too.*

It was as though they had been in separate worlds, but suddenly the future came together for them. Annamarie was sure God's voice would continue to lead them if they listened for it.

"Yes, Brad, forever."